KU-775-907

A TARGET ADVENTURE

DOCTOR WHO AND THE DOOMSDAY WEAPON

Based on the BBC television serial *Doctor Who and the Colony in Space* by Malcolm Hulke by arrangement with the British Broadcasting Corporation

MALCOLM HULKE

Illustrated by
Chris Achilleos

TARGET

a division of
Universal-Tandem Publishing Co., Ltd.,
14 Gloucester Road, London SW7 4RD

First published in Great Britain
by Universal-Tandem Publishing Co., Ltd., 1974

ISBN 0 426 10372 6

Printed in Great Britain by The Anchor Press Ltd., and bound
by Wm. Brendon & Son Ltd., both of Tiptree, Essex

CONTENTS

I

A Missing Secret

The young Time Lord sat at the side of the old Keeper of the Time Lords' Files at the control console. The old Keeper of the Files played his spindly fingers across the console's warmth-buttons: by touching the right combination of buttons he could project onto the screen before them any of the Time Lords' most secret files and records.

'These are the working-papers for the very first TARDIS,' the old Keeper said. He touched some warmth-buttons and the picture of a small square box showed on the screen. 'I often like to look at that, and to remember back into time.'

'Time has no meaning for us,' said the young Time Lord. 'It is neither forwards nor backwards.'

'For us as a species, no,' said the old Keeper. 'But for us as individuals there is a beginning, and, I regret, an end.' He spoke with feeling. He was now well over 2,000 years old. Soon this young Time Lord, a mere 573 years of age, would become the new Keeper of the Files.

The young Time Lord quickly changed the subject. 'The first TARDIS was very small,' he said.

'On the outside, yes,' said the old Keeper. 'Inside it could carry up to three persons, four with a squeeze. Later we built much bigger ones. There have been two stolen, you know.'

The young Time Lord didn't know. 'By our enemies?' he asked.

'No. By Time Lords. They both became bored with this place. It was too peaceful for them, not enough happening.' The old Keeper smiled to himself, as though remembering with some glee all the fuss when *two* TARDISes were stolen. 'One of them nowadays calls himself "the Doctor". The other says he is "the Master". The TARDIS stolen by the Doctor has a serious defect. Two defects, to be correct.'

'Then how was he able to get away with it?'

'Oh, it flew all right,' said the old Keeper. 'It could fly through Time and Space, through Matter and anti-Matter. But he can't direct it.'

'So he's lost in Time and Space?' asked the young Time Lord.

'Hardly.' The old Keeper was silent for a moment, and seemed almost about to drop off to sleep. The young Time Lord had become used to this and waited patiently. Suddenly the old Keeper's failing energies returned. 'Still, even if he cannot control it, others sometimes can.'

'I don't understand,' said the young Time Lord, 'what others? Who?'

'Who? No, Who can't control it . . . not always.' The old Keeper dropped his voice, and there was a faint smile on his 2,000-years-old lips. 'But others sometimes can.'

Obviously the question was not going to be answered. The young Time Lord hoped that eventually, perhaps in another thousand years, he would learn everything about the files and their secrets. For the time being though he had to be content with what the old Keeper cared to tell him.

'The other defect,' said the old Keeper, 'was that that particular TARDIS had lost its chameleon-like quality. It was in for repairs, you see—that's how the Doctor got his hands on it.'

'I don't understand about the chameleon quality,' said the young Time Lord, wishing he had taken over the job of the Files a few hundred years ago when the present Keeper was more lucid and awake and better able to explain things.

'It's a term we borrowed from a small, low-grade species of life on the planet Earth,' said the old Keeper, as though addressing a classroom. 'If a chameleon stands on the branch of a tree, it turns brown like the bark; but if it stands on a leaf, it turns green.'

'You mean TARDISes can change colour?'

'When they are working properly,' said the old Keeper, 'they change colour, shape, everything. From the beginning it was decided that a TARDIS must always look like something at home in its immediate background. You've never travelled, have you?'

'No, not yet.' The young Time Lord was a little ashamed to admit it.

'Pity. It broadens the mind.' The old Keeper seemed to drop off to sleep again for a moment, then he suddenly woke up with a start. 'I had to travel once. There were tens of thousands of humans from the planet Earth, stranded on another planet where they thought they were re-fighting all the wars of Earth's terrible history. The Doctor'—he interrupted himself—'I told you about him, didn't I?'

'Yes,' said the young Time Lord, now used to the old Keeper forgetting what he had already said. 'You mentioned the Doctor and the Master.'

'No, it wasn't the Master,' said the old Keeper in his confused way. 'The Master never does anything good for anyone. He's thoroughly evil. Now what was I saying?'

The Young Time Lord reminded him. 'Humans on a planet refighting the wars of Earth's history.'

'Oh, yes. Well, the Doctor had done the best he could to stop it all. But in the end we had to step in and get all those poor soldiers back to Earth, and to all the right times in Earth's history.'

'And is that when you travelled?'

'That's right,' said the old Keeper, his eyes bright now with the memory of his one and only trip away from the planet of the Time Lords. 'I and many others. When it landed, my TARDIS turned into a machine-gun post.'

'What's that?'

The old Keeper glanced at the young Time Lord.

'Oh, dear, you *have* a lot to learn.' He seemed to forget the question, and went on: 'Anyway, TARDISes are supposed to change colour and shape, but the one stolen by the Doctor stays all the time looking like a London police box.' Before the young Time Lord could speak, the old Keeper added quickly: 'And don't ask me what that is because I have no idea, not what they are for. Where were we?'

The young Time Lord indicated the small box on the screen. 'The working-papers for the original TARDIS.'

'Then that's enough of that,' said the old Keeper, taking his finger from the 'hold' button. Instantly, the picture on the screen vanished. 'It's time we had a break now, don't you think? I don't want to overwork you.'

'We've only just started this session of tuition,' said the young Time Lord. 'But if you're tired . . .'

The old Keeper sat up straight. 'Not at all!' He thrust a slender white hand into a pocket of his robe, fumbled about and brought out a scrap of paper. On it were mathematical symbols. 'I made some notes here of things you ought to know about. Let me see . . .' The young Time Lord watched as the old Keeper screwed up his watery eyes to read the symbols. 'Ah, yes,' said the old Keeper, 'the Doomsday Weapon. You must know about the Doomsday Weapon.' He put the scrap of paper back into his pocket, then spread both hands across the warmth-buttons.

The young Time Lord asked, 'I take it we have this weapon in safe keeping?'

'No,' said the old Keeper. 'It's not necessary. It is hidden on a distant and remote planet, a hiding-place known only to us.' He poised his fingers over a new combination of warmth-buttons.

'Why is it called Doomsday?'

'Because,' said the old Keeper, 'that is its name. Anybody controlling that terrible weapon could bring instant doom to large sections of the Universe. It radiates anti-Matter at a million times the speed of light.' He nodded his head at a button in the top left-hand corner of the console. 'Could you put your finger over that button, please. It's a safety measure, so that no one person with only two hands can activate the combination to produce the file on the Doomsday Weapon.'

The young Time Lord poised an index finger over the button.

'Now lower your finger,' said the old Keeper, 'as I lower mine.'

The old Keeper lowered his fingers onto a pattern of buttons, and the young Time Lord brought his index finger down gently onto the one remote button. Then they looked up at the screen. Printing appeared and it read: 'TOP SECRET. EXACT WHEREABOUTS OF THE DOOMSDAY WEAPON, AND INSTRUCTIONS FOR USE.'

'That's just the title-page of the file,' said the old Keeper. 'Move your finger to the next button on the right.'

The young Time Lord moved his index finger along to the adjacent button. Instantly, the printing disappeared and the screen went blank.

'All right,' said the old Keeper. 'Now touch the button.'

The young Time Lord touched the button. One line of bold handwriting appeared on the screen from the first inside page of the secret file. It said: '*Thank you for letting me know where to find the Doomsday Weapon. —The Master.*'

.   .   .   .   .

The three most superior Time Lords, known simply as the First, Second, and Third Time Lords, sat round a small oval table in their meeting-room. On the table before them was the report from the Keeper of the Files, which included the Master's message.

'At least the Master has a sense of humour,' said the Third Time Lord.

'He is also exceedingly dangerous and vicious,' said the Second Time Lord. 'If he finds the Doomsday

Weapon he can control the entire Universe through terror.'

The First Time Lord turned to a microphone set by his chair. 'Status report on the Master,' he said. Within a moment a voice answered from a loudspeaker in the ceiling above them.

'Last monitored on planet Earth,' said the voice. 'Late twentieth century Earth Time.'

'Earth?' said the Second Time Lord. 'Isn't that where we exiled the Doctor?'

'Yes,' said the First Time Lord, 'because he interfered too much in the destinies of other species.' He turned to the microphone again. 'Status report on the Doctor.'

The voice from the ceiling answered: 'Exiled to planet Earth by the High Tribunal, late twentieth century Earth Time.'

'I think,' said the First Time Lord, 'we might use the Doctor to deal with this problem.'

'Never,' said the Third Time Lord. 'He will not help us. He resents his exile too much.'

'That's true,' said the Second Time Lord. 'We also immobilised his TARDIS, taking away his freedom to move in Space and Time.'

'Then,' said the First Time Lord, 'we have no alternative but to restore his freedom.'

'Never!' exclaimed the Second Time Lord. 'If we seek his help he will hold it over us for ever more, and if we restore his freedom we shall have no control over him!'

The First Time Lord listened patiently to the outburst. Then he spoke quietly. 'We shall only let him *think* he is free again. We shall let his TARDIS fly, but only where we want it to fly.'

'What about afterwards?' asked the Third Time Lord.

'If the Doctor is unsuccessful,' said the First Time Lord, 'and is killed by the Master, or by those who protect the Doomsday Weapon, there will be no afterwards. Only time will tell.' He smiled at his own joke, and the other two Time Lords respectfully smiled with him.

2

Into Time and Space

Jo Grant squeezed her white mini between the Brigadier's big black staff-car and a military half-track vehicle in the UNIT car-park, got out and walked purposefully towards the main administration block. Overnight she had come to a big decision: either the Doctor must give her some work to do, or she was going to hand in her resignation.

It was really her uncle's fault. While still at school she decided what she most wanted to do: to become a spy. One half-term she took herself to London and sought out her uncle who worked as a Senior Civil Servant for the Government. 'I want to be a spy,' she said. He laughed, and sent out one of his many secretaries to buy her an ice-cream. 'There really *are* spies,' she insisted earnestly, 'and I want to be one.' She never knew whether her uncle took her completely seriously, or just wanted to please her, but the day she left school a letter arrived inviting her for an interview at the Security Training Establishment, somewhere in Surrey. She was accepted, and spent a year learning how to code and decode, how to speak two foreign languages, and how to read economic reports on wheat and oil production. At the end of the year she was given top marks, and told that her training was over. She was then offered a job as a filing clerk in the British Embassy in Bangkok.

Furious, Jo went to see her uncle again. 'I don't call *that* being a spy,' she complained. Her uncle tried to explain: most 'spying' in the world was carried on by clerks working in embassies; in fact most embassies, British and foreign, existed in order to send home reports on the economy of the country in which they were situated. It was dull, routine work. 'You should have explained that a year ago,' she said. 'I want an exciting job, and I don't mind if it's dangerous.' Her uncle thought for a moment, then said, 'How would you like to work for the United Nations Intelligence Taskforce?' She asked, 'What does it do?' 'Ah,' said the uncle, 'that's rather secret! But I'll have a word with Brigadier Lethbridge-Stewart. He's the man for you to see.'

A week later she was seated before the handsome Brigadier in his office at UNIT Headquarters. From the start of the interview she realised he didn't really want her on his staff. He was very polite, but it was clear he was only taking her on because her uncle had asked him. 'We have a chap here,' he said, 'called "the Doctor". He needs an assistant. That could be you.' She said, 'I don't know anything about medicine.' The Brigadier looked puzzled, then laughingly exclaimed: 'Oh, not *that* kind of Doctor. He's a scientist. You can start on Monday if you like.' With that the interview ended.

On the following Monday Jo reported for work and met the Doctor. He didn't seem at all impressed with her, and after a few minutes' talk about the weather he said he had important business elsewhere and hurried away. She didn't see him again for two days, during which period she wandered around the Headquarters to get to know it and the people who worked there.

On the Wednesday she found the Doctor again in what seemed to be a laboratory; for some reason an old-fashioned London police box stood in one corner. The Doctor was tinkering with some electrical gadget at a work bench. 'What are you doing?' said Jo. The Doctor looked up, and for the first time she saw that he had a very nice smile. 'I'd better explain,' he said; 'that's a Time and Space machine'—he indicated the old police box—'but it doesn't work at the moment. I'm trying to repair it.' Jo suddenly realised she had been given a job with a madman. 'Time and Space machine?' she laughed, not believing. The Doctor's smile faded quickly : 'I'll let you know if I need your assistance at any time. Good morning.' With that he turned back to the work bench. Jo still had nothing to do.

That was a week ago now. During the week she had mooned around the Headquarters, bored out of her mind. Now, today, she intended to have a showdown. Even being a filing clerk in the Embassy in Bangkok could be more interesting than reading magazines at UNIT Headquarters to kill time. As she entered the main building she passed Sergeant Benton, who gave her a friendly 'Good morning', but she was too angry to reply. She went straight down to the Doctor's laboratory. He was there, as always, tinkering with bits of wire on the work bench.

'I must speak to you,' she said. 'I'm supposed to work for you, but you don't give me anything to do!'

'Just a moment, my dear.' The Doctor seemed to apply himself to some task requiring great concentration. Jo looked and saw he was soldering two bits of wire together—nothing more complicated.

'Look,' she said, 'what *is* that thing you're working on?'

'It's a new dematerialisation circuit,' he said. He had by now successfully joined together the two bits of wire. 'There! That bit's done.' He straightened up and looked pleased with himself.

'Dematerialisation?' queried Jo. 'Of what?'

'The TARDIS,' said the Doctor, as if Jo ought to understand.

Jo was completely puzzled. 'What sort of Doctor are you?' she asked.

'What sort would you like me to be?' the Doctor replied.

Before Jo could make a retort, the Brigadier had entered. 'Oh, 'morning, Miss Grant,' he said, acknowledging her existence for the first time in a week; then he turned to the Doctor. 'I've just got the latest field reports about the Master. There's no trace of him.'

'As I expected,' said the Doctor. 'His TARDIS is working now, remember. He could be anywhere in Space and Time.'

'That's as may be,' said the Brigadier. 'But I'm going to keep on looking.'

'You're wasting your time,' said the Doctor.

Jo looked from one of the men to the other as they talked, with as much understanding as a cat watching a ball bounced between two table-tennis players. She had never heard of 'the Master', nor did she know what 'TARDIS' meant. Then she realised that the work bench 'phone was ringing, and since the other two were deep in this mysterious conversation she picked it up to answer—the first act of work since she had joined UNIT.

'Hello?'

A man's voice asked for the Brigadier. Jo gave the 'phone to Lethbridge-Stewart, and he had a quickfire conversation with the caller. Then he cradled the 'phone, and turned back to the Doctor. He seemed very pleased.

'One of our agents thinks he's traced the Master,' said the Brigadier. 'I hope to be back here within the hour with good news. Excuse me.'

The Brigadier hurried out. The Doctor watched after him, shaking his head sadly.

'Can't you tell me *anything* that's going on?' asked Jo. 'Who is the Master, and what's a TARDIS?'

'Didn't the Brigadier explain it all to you?' said the Doctor.

'No,' said Jo. 'No one's explained anything.'

'Oh dear,' the Doctor said. 'Well, the Master is a fellow we've had quite a bit of trouble with. As for TARDIS, that means Time And Relative Dimensions in Space.' The Doctor ended there with a smile, as though he had explained everything.

'Time and Relative Dimensions . . .' said Jo. 'You mean *that* thing?' She pointed to the old police box.

'That *thing*,' said the Doctor, obviously a little hurt,

'is probably the most advanced technological device you will ever encounter in your entire life.'

Jo went over and inspected the police box. 'It looks just like an old police box to me.'

'I see,' said the Doctor, clearly not very pleased with Jo's attitude. 'Since I'm about to go inside I'll let you see for yourself.' The Doctor picked up the electrical gadget he had been working on, crossed to the police box and produced a key. He unlocked the little narrow door, and threw it open. 'After you.'

Jo looked inside, expecting to see a poky little space perhaps with a police telephone and a first-aid box. Inside she found herself looking into a huge, futuristic-looking control room.

She turned back to the Doctor : 'It's a trick. An optical illusion.'

'Why not step inside and see?' said the Doctor.

Cautiously, Jo entered the TARDIS. It was at least twenty times bigger inside than outside. She stood just inside, unable to speak. The Doctor, however, followed her in and immediately went to a central console in the middle of the vast, highly polished floor. Without a word he set about inserting his bit of electrical gadgetry into a cavity in the console.

At last Jo got her voice back. 'How can it be bigger inside than out?'

'The TARDIS is dimensionally transcendental,' said the Doctor, busy with his work. Whatever he was doing, he seemed satisfied with his own work. He straightened up. 'As of this moment,' he said, 'I think my exile on Earth may be over.'

'Your exile on Earth?' Jo was seriously worried about this strange man's sanity. 'If you don't mind,' she said, 'I think I'll be getting along.' She turned on her heel to leave, only to find that the huge metallic doors were just closing in front of her. She swung back to the Doctor. 'Kindly open these doors immediately, Doctor! The joke's over.'

Now the Doctor loooked at the doors. A smile spread

across his face. 'I don't think I'll be able to,' he said. 'We're taking off!'

Jo crossed to the big doors, now firmly closed. 'Open these doors, Doctor!'

The Doctor suddenly seemed to realise that Jo was really terrified and that he should do something. He went to the central console, pulled a small lever, then looked to the doors. 'I'm very sorry,' he said, 'but things seem to be out of my control. You'd better hold on to something tight.'

Even before he had completed the sentence, the floor of the control room started to vibrate violently, then to heave from side to side like a ship at sea. At the same time, Jo's ears were pierced by a terrifying sound, something like, yet not quite like, the trumpeting of a thousand mad elephants. Jo reeled across the floor, grabbed at a metal support pillar and clung on for dear life. Her arms locked round the support pillar, she felt violently sick, her mind filled with the noise and the heaving of the floor beneath her. Then black clouds filled her mind, and she was just aware of slowly sinking to the floor, her arms still locked round the pillar.

3
The Planet

'I'm sorry, but I don't remember your name.'

Jo heard the Doctor's voice coming to her as though from a far distance. Slowly she opened her eyes. She was on the floor of the TARDIS, her arms still locked firmly round the base of the pillar. The Doctor was kneeling over her.

'Jo Grant,' she said, automatically. 'Call me Jo.'

'Let me help you up, Jo,' said the Doctor. He put his hands under her arms to lift her. For a moment Jo let him, then, with returning strength, she got herself up.

'Open those doors, please.' Jo tried to sound very cold, like one of the teachers she had known and hated at school. 'The joke's over, Doctor.'

'First,' the Doctor said, crossing back to the central console, 'we must check if it's safe.'

'It's perfectly safe to open those doors,' said Jo, keeping well away from him. 'I intend to go straight to the Brigadier and offer my resignation.' Within a week, she had decided, she would be on a plane to Bangkok, or wherever jobs were going for Embassy filing clerks.

But the Doctor was taking no notice of her. Instead, he was gazing in wonder at a monitor screen set in the wall of the control room. 'Look,' he said. 'Just look at that.'

Jo looked. The monitor screen showed a barren landscape, a treeless stretch of rock and occasional shrubs. 'It looks like somewhere in North Wales,' she said, trying to humour him. 'Now please open the doors.'

'But don't you realise,' he said, 'that's what's outside. I must check the temperature and the atmosphere be-

19

fore we open those doors.' The Doctor busied himself reading dials set in the control console. 'Good,' he said at last. 'Very similar to Earth.'

'No little green men with two heads?' queried Jo, sarcastically, still keeping her distance from the Doctor.

The Doctor looked again at the monitor screen. 'Not so far as I can see. Actually, two-headed species in the

'No little green men with two heads?' queried Jo sarcastically.

Cosmos are very rare. There are the Deagles, a sort of two-headed birdlike creature, on one of the planets in the Asphasian Belt, but I've only read about those. I haven't been there yet . . .'

Jo cut in: 'Just open the doors, please!' She stood with her back pressed against the doors, to keep as far as possible from this raving lunatic called the Doctor.

'Certainly,' he said. 'I hope we're going to find it interesting.'

The Doctor operated the small lever. Jo could just hear the doors opening behind her. She remained facing the Doctor, not daring to take her eyes off him in case he went suddenly mad and tried to attack her. Only when she was sure that the doors were fully open, allowing her to make a quick run for it up to the Brigadier's office, did she turn. And then she saw the barren landscape that lay outside. Her heart pounded. She couldn't utter a sound.

'Well?' said the Doctor, coming up behind her. 'Shall we investigate?'

Without waiting for an answer, the Doctor strode outside. A keen wind ruffled his hair. He stood there, breathing deeply, clearly very happy. Then he looked back at Jo. 'Shall we take a walk?'

Jo stepped outside. As she did so, she turned back to look at the TARDIS. It was the same police box she had seen in the Doctor's laboratory. 'Where are we?'

'No idea,' said the Doctor. 'Anywhere, and any time, in the Cosmos. I suggest that we take a quick look round; then I'll try to get you back to Earth.'

'We're not on Earth?'

'I rather doubt it.' The Doctor stood surveying the landscape of rock and occasional shrub. Then he spotted something on the horizon. 'No,' he said, 'definitely not Earth. Look over there.'

Jo looked to the horizon, and saw two bright white discs in the sky. 'What are they?'

'Moons,' he said. 'Planet Earth has only one. This planet has those two, possibly more. So we're certainly not on Earth.' He stopped short, his keen eyes looking at something on the ground a few yards away. 'It's inhabited!' He hurried across to the point he had noticed. 'On the ground here,' he called back to Jo, 'tracks made by some kind of machine.' He inspected the tracks, then stood up straight and looked all around. 'Let's go up there,' he called. 'We'll get a better view. Come on!'

The Doctor strode off towards a small hill. Jo had had enough of all this. She turned to go back inside the TARDIS. The door was closed. She tried it, but it was locked. 'Doctor,' she called, 'come and open this door at once!' But the Doctor was already out of earshot, half way up the slaggy little hill. In sudden anger Jo raced after him, stumbling over the rocks. 'Doctor,' she called as she ran, 'I think this is all some big trick. You hypnotised me, and now you're making me think I'm on another planet!' At last she was up beside him. 'Do you hear me! I want to go home!'

But the Doctor was gazing in wonder into the distance. 'Look over there, Jo.' He pointed to a valley now visible from the hilltop. In the valley was a dome-shaped object as big as a very large house, and next to it what might be a spaceship. The dome and the spaceship were about two miles away from where they stood. 'We could easily walk over there,' the Doctor said with almost childlike enthusiasm. 'It wouldn't take more than an hour.'

Jo said, 'I want to go back to your TARDIS.'

'But Jo, there may be some different life form over there, something neither of us has ever seen before in our lives, and will never see again.' There was pleading in the Doctor's voice.

'Have you really done this sort of thing before?' asked Jo. She was beginning to feel less scared of the Doctor, even a little sorry for him.

'What?' he said, as though his interest had suddenly darted off in another direction. He had picked up a small piece of rock and was examining it with great curiosity.

'This space travelling,' said Jo. 'Have you done this before?'

'For years I roamed the Universe,' he said. 'Then the Time Lords cought me, exiled me to Earth, and immobilised my TARDIS. You see, I don't really want to work for UNIT. I want to be free.' He paused, looking up from the piece of rock in his hand. 'We could get to that valley in an hour or so, have a look round, and then go back to TARDIS and get back to Earth. What do you say?'

Jo gave in. 'All right. But I still don't believe any of this is really happening. I expect to wake up any moment and find—'

'*Stand where you are!*'

The gruff male voice shouted from behind them. Both the Doctor and Jo remained absolutely still.

'One move,' said the voice, 'and I'll shoot!'

Jo heard the man's booted feet on the rocks as he circled round them. She didn't even dare to move her head to look at him. The man circled them at a distance to bring himself facing them. He was a rough-looking man wearing heavy boots, blue denims, and an old battered hat. He held a futuristic-looking shotgun, which he kept trained on the Doctor and Jo.

'Inspecting rock samples, eh?' said the man.

'What?' The Doctor looked at the piece of rock in his hand. 'Oh, yes. Could you point that gun the other way?'

'Bit of prospecting, eh?' said the man, more as a statement than a question.

'Is there anything to prospect for?' asked the Doctor.

The man gestured with his gun. 'Start moving.'

'That's most kind of you,' the Doctor said. 'You see we have our means of transport not far from here. Come along, Jo.' He grabbed Jo's hand, and turned in the direction of the TARDIS.

'Not that way!' said the man. 'Straight ahead. I'm taking you in as prisoners.'

'We haven't done anything wrong,' Jo said. 'We don't even want to be here.'

'Move,' said the man, 'or I shoot.'

'I think we must do what he wants,' the Doctor said. 'This way, Jo.'

Jo clung to the Doctor's hand as they moved forward. The man followed behind, his gun on their backs all the time. Despite the Doctor's efforts, he refused to be drawn into conversation. He only spoke to tell them to

23

bear a bit more to the left or the right. First they went downhill, away from the TARDIS, then up another very small hill. When they reached the crest of this hill they saw before them a small dome surrounded by crude fencing. This clearly was their destination, and the Doctor strode towards it with Jo still clinging to his hand. As Jo got closer she could see that the dome was made of moulded metal sheets, and that the structure had a door and windows. It looked very futuristic, yet the fence running round the 'garden' consisted of crudely hacked tree branches, as one might have seen on Earth in the Middle Ages.

'Go in,' said the man.

The Doctor and Jo entered the dome. It was very simply furnished—just an old bed, a rough kitchen table, some hardback chairs. A woman dressed in a long skirt and blue denim shirt was cooking something, using a portable infra-red oven. Her simple clothes were faded and had been patched many times.

'Good afternoon,' said the Doctor.

The woman spun round in astonishment.

The man followed them inside, still keeping his gun trained on them. 'I found them spying in Sector 27,' he told the woman, who was obviously his wife. 'Cover them.'

Without a word the woman took a shotgun from the wall, and aimed it at Jo and the Doctor. Now the man put down his gun. 'Hands above your heads,' he said 'I want your weapons.'

'We have no weapons,' the Doctor said. 'And why do you have guns? Who are you afraid of?'

But the man didn't answer. He crossed to the Doctor, and felt his pockets for concealed arms. Satisfied that he had none, he turned his attention to Jo.

'You're not touching *me*,' said Jo.

'Maybe not,' said the man. He turned to his wife. 'Keep an eye on them. I'll radio-telephone Ashe, and tell him that I'm bringing them in.' He went to a corner of the one main room, sat himself before a radio-telephone, put on earphones and quietly had a conversation with whomever he was calling.

'I asked,' said the Doctor, 'why you have guns?'

'The Primitives,' said the woman. 'We heard a band of them roaming about in this area.'

'Are they the original inhabitants of this planet?' the Doctor asked.

She said, 'Didn't they tell you?'

'Didn't who tell me?' asked the Doctor.

'The combine that you're working for,' she said.

'We're not working for anybody,' said the Doctor.

'Then who sent you?' she said.

'No one,' said the Doctor. 'We came here of our own accord. We're from the planet Earth.'

'This is *our* planet,' said the woman. 'We don't need any more settlers.'

'Settlers?' said the Doctor. 'We're not settlers. We are explorers.'

The man returned from the radio-telephone and heard what the Doctor said: 'So you admit it! You're explorers, prospecting for one of the mining combines!' He turned to his wife. 'Ashe says for me to take them to the main dome right away.' He picked up his gun, trained it on the Doctor. 'Right! Move! And you, too, Miss!'

Jo said, 'I do wish you'd let us explain.'

'You can do your explaining at the main dome,' the man replied. 'On your way, now! And if either of you try to run for it, I'll kill you both.' He turned to his wife: 'You come too, and bring your gun.'

Nothing was said during the second part of their journey, except for an occasional 'Move to the right' or 'Move to the left' from the man behind them with the gun. All the ground they covered was rocky and bare, although once Jo saw a pretty little flower with alternate red and blue petals—something she could never see on Earth. But she thought it best not to stop to inspect the flower; the man with the gun might have fired instantly. After four or five little hills they came into sight again of the big dome with its spaceship. Being closer now to the spaceship she could see that it was rather battered in appearance, and some lettering on its side had been partly burned off so that she could not make out any of the words.

'In there?' the Doctor asked, not turning his head but indicating the main entrance to the dome.

'In there,' said the voice behind them.

Jo and the Doctor went into the main dome, the man and woman following them. The man said, 'Stop where you are.'

They halted, and Jo looked round the inside of the main dome. They were in a large room that formed only part of the interior of the dome; corridors led off to other parts. Different from the exterior of the dome, with its futuristic sheets of gleaming moulded metal, the inside was more like a barn. There were plastic crates stored in one corner, and bits of agricultural machinery stacked in another. The floor was untidy with bits of mud and straw brought in on the boots of the people who came in and out of the building which was, in effect, the meeting-place of some community. And now, as they entered and stopped, a meeting was in progress. A big, white-haired man, clearly the leader, was listening to a man and woman who seemed very upset and worried. Standing about, listening, were other men and women. They all wore clothes similar to those of the man standing now behind Jo and the Doctor with his gun—simple farm workers' denims and heavy boots, with all the women and girls in long skirts.

'Now you listen to me, Ashe,' said the worried-looking man, 'I saw those creatures. Both me and my wife saw them, with our own eyes!'

The big man with white hair, called Ashe, tried to look calm. 'I surveyed this planet myself before the colony was set up. There was no trace of hostile animal life.'

Now the worried-looking woman spoke up. 'We heard this roaring in the middle of the night. When we looked out, there it was.

One of the younger men present asked a question. 'What did it look like?'

'It was enormous,' the woman said. 'Some kind of giant lizard.'

Ashe asked calmly, 'Did it do any damage?'

'Well, no,' the worried-looking man replied, 'I took a few shots at it and frightened it away.'

'You've been having nightmares!' the younger man retorted. 'Too much rich food!'

All the people grinned, but it wasn't a happy grin. Jo realised that the young man had made some joke that they all understood. Then she noticed how thin they all were, and how threadbare were their clothes. These people were all poor, just clinging on to an existence on this strange planet. The leader, Ashe, now noticed the Doctor and Jo and the man and woman who had brought them here.

'All right, Leeson,' said Ashe, 'what's your problem? More monsters?'

'I found these two in Sector 27,' said Leeson, still keeping his gun trained on Jo and the Doctor. 'They *say* they are explorers.'

'I'll deal with them in a moment,' said Ashe. He turned back to the worried-looking man and woman who had been talking about monsters. 'Why don't you two go and have something to eat, and a rest? You must be tired after walking all the way here.'

'We've got to find the creature and kill it,' the man said. He turned to the younger man, the one who had made the joke. 'Winton, you're in charge of the guards. It's your job to go and kill this thing, not to make jokes. It's bad enough trying to scratch a living on this planet without being pestered by giant lizards in the middle of the night!'

An older woman stepped forward to the couple who had seen the monster. 'You could both do with something to eat. Come along with me.'

'All right,' said the man, 'for my wife's sake. But we've got to *do* something. The crops won't grow, and the

Primitives aren't all that friendly. If we've also got to fight off monsters, my vote is that we all go back to where we came from!'

The man's wife tugged at his sleeve, and reluctantly he went with her down one of the corridors. Ashe turned to the young man, Winton. 'How many men can you raise?'

'Here at the main dome,' Winton said, 'maybe half-a-dozen. The rest are on outpost guard.'

'Half-a-dozen will have to do,' said Ashe. 'Put a guard on the Martins' dome, just in case.'

'Right,' said Winton, and hurried away.

Ashe came over to the Doctor and Jo and the man called Leeson. 'Where do you two come from?'

'Earth,' said the Doctor. 'You seem to have problems here.'

'I caught them examining rock samples,' said Leeson. 'They're mineralogists. It was bound to happen. I said from the start they'd never leave us in peace.'

Jo was confused with what Leeson was saying. Who wouldn't leave them in peace?—and what was *bound* to happen? But she thought it best to say nothing. If life had been boring working for UNIT, it certainly wasn't dull now.

'Look,' the Doctor was saying, 'I'm not a professional mineralogist. But suppose I were? Why all the hostility?'

'Because,' said Ashe, 'we don't want our planet gutted.'

'This is *our* world,' said Mrs. Leeson, speaking up for almost the first time, her gun still trained on Jo and the Doctor. 'You've no right to be here!'

Now Jo couldn't contain herself any longer: 'Would someone please explain what all this is about?'

'Yes, indeed,' said the Doctor. 'Surely you could explain to us what we're being accused of doing?'

'This planet,' said Ashe, 'has been classified as suitable for colonisation. That means farming, so far as we're concerned. But if the big mining companies move in they'll turn it into a galactic slag heap in no time.'

'Don't you have any rights?' asked the Doctor.

'The big mining companies don't bother about people's rights,' said Leeson, full of bitterness. 'They move in, rip the minerals out of a planet, and move on somewhere else. It happened to the planet we got our seed from!'

'We're not sure of that,' said Ashe. 'We only know that their radio stopped working.'

'Yes?' said Leeson. 'And what about their final message?'

'Do excuse me,' said the Doctor, 'but I don't understand what you're talking about.'

Ashe turned to the Doctor to explain. 'With no land farming on Earth, we had to get seed from somewhere to start farming here. So on the way we stopped at another colonised planet, and traded for seed. Once we got here we kept up radio contact with those colonists for a while. They were very useful, giving us advice. Then after some months they radio'd through and a voice said: "The miners are here—" and cut out. We never heard from them again.'

'Because they were probably all killed!' said Leeson hotly. He turned back to the Doctor. 'If it happens here and we even have time to complain to Earth Government, there'll be no decision from Earth till the miners have finished their job. There won't be anything left to have rights about!'

'That's terrible,' said the Doctor. 'But I do assure you, I and my young companion aren't working for anybody. Our spaceship developed a fault and we had to land somewhere. I'm very sorry that we've intruded.'

Ashe asked, 'Can you show me your identification?'

'Identification?' said the Doctor, taken off guard by this question. 'Oh, that's back in my spaceship. If we could go back there—'

But Ashe cut in: 'I think it better if you two stay the night. It'll be dark outside by now. We'll visit your ship in the morning.'

Jo had no wish to stay in this grim-looking barn for

the night. 'We don't want to put you to any trouble,' she said. 'We're quite willing to go now, and find our own way.'

'As you heard,' said Ashe, 'two of our colonists believe they saw some hostile creatures abroad last night. We must all be very careful.'

'We'll come to no harm,' said Jo. 'We can look after ourselves. Can't we, Doctor?'

She looked up to the Doctor, hoping for agreement. Instead he was looking straight ahead at Ashe. 'We shall be glad to stay,' he said.

Jo tugged at his sleeve, 'But Doctor . . .'

He turned and gave her a look that clearly meant, *'Shut up and leave this to me!'*

Ashe turned to one of the younger women who was watching, a girl so like him in her looks that clearly she was his daughter. 'Mary, why don't you take our guests to the dining-hall? And arrange some sleeping quarters for them.'

The girl called Mary nodded, and smiled at Jo. 'We have a little food,' she said. 'You're welcome to share it. Come.' She held out her hand for Jo to take it.

Jo looked from the Doctor to Ashe and to the Leesons, all of whom were now looking at her. 'All right,' she said at last, 'we'll stay just this one night. Coming to supper, Doctor?'

'Shortly,' said the Doctor. 'There are things I wish to discuss here.'

Jo realised there was no point in arguing. She took hold of Mary's hand and allowed herself to be taken down one of the corridors. It was dimly lit, but the lights were electric. 'Where do you get your electrical power?' she asked the girl.

'The spaceship,' said Mary. 'The main dome is linked to its generators. This is our dining-hall.'

Jo was led into a room with a single long table, on either side of which were long benches. Like the few items of furniture in the Leesons' little dome, the table and benches were poorly made with rough surfaces. Jo sat to the table, while Mary went to ladle thick soup from a big black cauldron that stood on a small electric ring. Mary brought the soup to Jo and gave her a roughly-made wooden spoon.

'I'm afraid that's all we can offer,' Mary said. 'It's not very much, is it?'

Jo looked into the soup. It seemed to contain root vegetables. 'It looks very nice,' she said. Then she tried some. It had almost no taste. 'It's marvellous,' she lied.

'I'm glad you like it,' said Mary, and sat down beside Jo. She looked at Jo's clothes. 'Is that what they're wearing on Earth now?'

'More or less,' said Jo.

'Things change so quickly,' Mary sighed. 'It was all quite different when we left back in 'seventy-one.'

'You left Earth in nineteen seventy-one?' Jo asked. By 1971 only a handful of astronauts had travelled beyond Earth, and then only for very short spells on the Moon.

Mary laughed. 'You're a bit out with your time,' she said. 'Two thousand nine hundred and seventy-one—that's when we left, just a year ago.'

'You mean the date is now 2972?'

'That's right,' said Mary, 'of course it is.'

Jo realised that she had not only travelled through Space; she had also travelled through one thousand years of Time!

4
The Monster

Jane Leeson trudged through the darkness by the side of her husband. The gun she carried weighed heavily in the crook of her arm, and she wondered if she would ever get used to having to carry it every time she left their dome.

'Who do you think those people really are?' she asked her husband.

'I don't know,' he said. 'Ashe will sort it out.' He walked a little faster, so that Jane had to hurry over the broken rocks to keep up. It was his way of showing that he didn't want to talk.

She thought back on the life they had had together on Earth. From the history books and the history films, she had learned of a time when there were open spaces on Earth, when both people and animals could roam free in great areas of grass and trees. But Earth hadn't been like that for hundreds of years. Every square kilometre of land had been built over, with roads and monorails over-running the great sprawling built-up areas. This area, which extended everywhere, was twenty to thirty storeys deep, with linking corridors and escalatorways so that people could go shopping and get to work—all under cover, with fresh air sucked in by huge ventilators from above. As a special treat, on nonwork days, you could pay to go up to the surface in an elevator and spend a few hours sitting on concrete in the sunshine. Another treat was to go for a Walk. This meant you paid to go into a special cubicle with a floor that rolled from one end of the cubicle to another. To stay in one place you had to keep walking. Meanwhile, all around you, there was a moving picture on the walls of passing grass and trees, and sometimes wild animals, films that came from the State Archives. To further the illusion they blew gusts of fresh air at you, sometimes with funny smells that were supposed to resemble those of animals and grass.

She met her husband during such a Walk. The roller had jerked suddenly, owing to a power failure, and she had fallen over. Leeson helped her to her feet, and so they met. By getting married they qualified for a room of their own. Previously she had had to share a room with her parents and three sisters. The marriage was conducted by a friendly computer that played music to them as well as announcing that their State records had been stapled together in the great Automatic State Personnel File, which meant they were then married. Then the computer gave them the key to their room, a cubicle just big enough for a double-bed, a shower, and a lavatory. They took one look at the room and decided they had to escape.

In the old days, between five hundred and a thousand years ago, people had escaped from the towns by going to the country. But there was no country now. Instead, groups of people clubbed together and bought up old spaceships and went to the planets. For the next six years Jane and her husband worked hard and saved their money. Not once did they go up in the lifts for a sunshine treat, or even for a Walk treat. At the end of this time they reckoned they had enough money put by and started to read advertisements from people getting together colonist groups. The advertisement they answered was from Ashe. He had already travelled in Space on one of Earth's astro-merchant-ships, and he knew of a planet not dissimilar from Earth which had been classified for colonisation. It was uninhabited, Ashe said, except for a few Primitives who, if handled properly, would be no trouble. A meeting was held, and the Leesons met the other people who had answered Ashe's advertisement. They pooled their savings with the others, and then raided their local library for old books on what was known as farming. Meanwhile Ashe found a fairly good secondhand spaceship, and organised the making of agricultural machinery based on pictures in old books about land farming. Eventually the great day arrived, and all the would-be colonists boarded the spaceship and they travelled to this awful planet.

Because, in Jane's troubled mind, this planet *was* awful. Certainly there was room to move, and for the first few days the weary travellers from Earth did nothing but walk around in huge circles, shout, and literally fling their arms about. The main dome, brought in sections in the spaceship's vast hold, was put up first: it provided temporary quarters for all of them, plus a permanent meeting-place, and a home for John Ashe and his daughter. Then they all helped each other to put up the small single-family domes, all some distance from the main dome in the centre of the land which now belonged to the various couples and families. After that they had to sow the seed they had brought, and then live on iron-rations until the seed grew. But the seed did not grow. If it grew at all, it quickly withered and died. Ashe, who had made himself expert in book-learnt agriculture, spent day and night analysing soil samples and trying to work out which fertilisers should be used where. But nothing made any difference.

Meanwhile, there came the news about the big mineralogical combines from Earth gutting other planets, some of them with colonists already there. Earth's mineral resources had been used up hundreds of years ago, forcing Man to seek his needs on other planets. The big mining companies had built great fleets of spaceships, manned by ruthless mercenaries who were quite capable of plundering a planet already successfully colonised by farmers, ruining the land, killing and maiming people who tried to stand up for their rights. If Earth Government took any action at all, it was almost always too late.

Now, on top of all their other fears and hardships,

34

these other colonists, the Martins, had been attacked by monsters. One thing Ashe had promised about the planet was that it contained no hostile life forms. Jane had heard of some of the terrifying creatures space-travellers had found over the centuries—Monoids, Drahvins, some small metallic creatures called Daleks, and even from the bowels of Earth there had emerged once a race of reptile men.* This planet was big, as large as Earth itself, and it was foolish of them to believe Ashe when he had said that there were no hostile life forms. How could one man know what lay over the horizon, perhaps hundreds or thousands of kilometres away?—something that had now become attracted to the humans' colony?

As they neared the single dome, Jane spoke her mind. 'I want to go back to Earth.'

Her husband kept on walking. 'How?'

It was a sensible question. The spaceship belonged to all of them; it couldn't be used by one couple who wanted to return to Earth. She said: 'We should have a meeting, and see how many others feel like me. Those who want to stay can do so. Those who want to go have a right to take the spaceship.'

Now they had reached their dome and were going inside. 'We'll talk about it in the morning,' said Leeson.

'I want to talk about it now,' she said. 'We should never have come here.'

Leeson took her gun, hung it in its place on the wall. 'On Earth we had one room. Here we own land.'

'Land that grows nothing,' she exclaimed bitterly. 'Ashe knows we're beaten, and so do you. You just won't admit it.'

But Leeson wasn't listening to her. He was standing in the middle of their room, listening intently to something outside. He put his fingers to his lips to tell Jane to be quiet. From somewhere she could hear a low growling sound.

'You get on the radio,' ordered Leeson. 'I'm going outside.'

35

*The door was filled with something infinitely more terrifying than
she had ever imagined in her wildest dreams.*

'No, please,' his wife implored. 'Stay here!'

There was another growl, this time much louder and closer.

'I might be able to frighten it off,' said Leeson. 'Now do as you're told!' Without another word Leeson walked back into the night outside. Almost instantly there was a roar from the darkness beyond, the sort of sound Jane had only ever heard before from the films during a Walk on Earth when you saw non-existent animals called elephants and lions.

Jane went to the radio-telephone, put on the earphones, took up the microphone and pressed the transmitting button. 'Hello, main dome. Can you hear me? Can you hear me?'

Within a few moments Mary Ashe's voice came through the earphones. 'This is main dome. Please identify.'

'This is Jane Leeson. Our dome's being attacked! Please you must send help . . .'

Jane stopped as she heard from outside a human scream rend the air, unmistakably that of her husband. She dropped the earphones and rushed to the door to go out. But the door was already filled with something infinitely more terrifying than she had ever imagined in her wildest dreams.

Jane retreated backwards into the room. 'No,' she whispered, finding it almost impossible to speak. 'Do you understand what I say? Please don't touch me. I'll do anything . . . We'll go away . . . We'll leave the planet— all of us! But *please* don't kill me!'

Then she fainted.

---

* See DOCTOR WHO AND THE CAVE-MONSTERS.

5

Starvation

After Jo had been taken to supper by Mary Ashe, and the Leesons had gone back to their dome, the Doctor spent some time with Ashe discussing the colonists' basic problem—how to make their crops grow. Ashe, a reasonable man, accepted the Doctor's story that he and Jo were simply travellers in space, and had nothing to do with the mining combines that the colonists feared so much.

'What convinced you,' asked the Doctor, 'that crops would grow on this planet?'

'I visited this planet when I was a member of the crew of an astro-merchant-ship,' said Ashe. 'It has atmosphere that humans can breathe, and a temperature that humans can tolerate with comfort. The soil was exhausted, but I decided it could be reclaimed.'

'How?'

'Plant a cover crop,' Ashe said, 'plough it in, and repeat the process. That way we should have had a subsistence crop within a year. But even the cover crop refuses to grow.'

'What exhausted the soil originally?' asked the Doctor.

Ashe shrugged. 'The Primitives, I suppose. Before they *were* Primitives.'

The Doctor asked Ashe to tell him about the people called 'the Primitives'. Ashe explained that they were a simple people, similar to humans except for their six-fingered hands. 'They don't wear any clothes at all,' said

Ashe, 'which shocked some of our lady colonists a bit at first. Instead, they paint their bodies all over with dyes that they make somehow from the rocks.'

The Doctor asked, 'What do they live on?'

'The shrubs,' replied Ashe. 'I think they're half-starved most of the time. They're just clinging to existence. But they're not a people struggling to develop. They're going backwards.'

The Doctor found this intriguing. 'What makes you say that?'

'Wait till you see them,' said Ashe. 'Oh, don't worry, they carry spears but they're pretty harmless if you treat them gently. At least, that's how I've found them. Now about going backwards . . . Although they don't wear clothes, they wear belts and necklaces, sometimes arm bands, and these are always decorated with bits of machinery.

'What sort of machinery?'

'Shaped bits of metal,' said Ashe, 'that must have come from something. Maybe nuts, or bolts, or springs, or—just shaped bits of metal.'

The Doctor asked where the Primitives lived. Ashe explained that, so far as he knew, they lived in caves. 'You're fairly safe with them,' Ashe said reassuringly, 'so long as you don't go near their caves. That's when they get nasty. Then, and if ever they see a child's doll.'

'Dolls make them nasty?' asked the Doctor, even more intrigued.

'One of them was in here one day,' said Ashe, 'scrounging food, and my daughter happened to bring a little doll—one she'd had since she was a child—from her belongings. The Primitive almost went mad . . .'

And it was at this point that Mary Ashe came rushing back, accompanied by Jo, with the news of Jane Leeson's radio message. 'All she said was, "Our dome's being attacked. Please you must send help." Then she cut off.'

'Did she say what was attacking them?' asked the Doctor.

'No,' said Mary, near to tears. 'But I could hear by her voice—it was something awful.'

'I'll get my gun,' said Ashe, and started to move off to one of the corridors.

'Don't you need to go with other men?' Jo asked.

Ashe paused. 'We've sent the other men to the Martin's place. That's the other end of the colony. You all stay here.' With, that, Ashe hurried away.

The Doctor turned to Mary Ashe. 'Could this be Primitives attacking?'

Mary shook her head. 'No, I don't think so. We get on with the Primitives quite well.'

'Except,' said the Doctor, 'when one of them saw a doll of yours.'

Mary had to think back. 'Oh, that was ages ago. Yes, he got very excited and wanted to take it from me. I let him. That seemed to make him happy.'

'What did he do with it?' the Doctor asked.

'Held it to himself,' Mary said, 'as if to protect it from *me*, of all people. Then he ran away with it.'

Ashe returned carrying one of the futuristic-looking shotguns. 'I'll go to the Leesons' place as fast as I can,' he told Mary. 'You get on the radio and see if you can get anyone else to go over there—armed.'

'I shall go with you,' said the Doctor.

'No, Doctor,' said Jo. 'It may be dangerous.'

'A very good reason for going,' the Doctor said. He turned to Ashe. 'Are you ready?'

Ashe thought for a moment. 'All right. But at your own risk, mind. Now Mary, get on that radio!'

The Doctor followed Ashe out into the darkness. The clear night sky was bright with stars, not all like white pinhead dots as seen from Earth but some close enough to appear as small discs of intense light. With such a radiant night sky it was easy to see the shapes of the hills all around the main dome. Ashe strode ahead in a dead straight line for the Leesons' dome. He said not a word to the Doctor as he went ahead purposefully. Finally, they came to the crest of a little rocky hill and Ashe paused to look down. In the valley a few hundred yards ahead of them they saw two or three lights moving about, the flashlights of other men who had arrived there first.

'We aren't alone!' Ashe charged down the hill towards the lights, calling: 'Hello! Is everything all right?'

The Doctor ran after Ashe, taking care not to trip and fall headlong on to the rocky uninviting ground. When he came up with Ashe just outside the little dome, Ashe was staring at something on the ground. Another man was standing close by; it was the young man called Winton whom the Doctor had seen at the meeting in the main dome. Winton had a torch in his hand.

'It's no good,' Winton was saying, 'he's dead.'

'I want to see,' Ashe said.

Winton pointed his torch at the object on the ground. It was Leeson's body. The face and chest had been hacked as though by knives. There was blood everywhere. Winton switched off his torch.

'What about the woman?' asked the Doctor.

'The same,' said Winton. 'They're bringing her body out now.'

Ashe stood staring at the form lying on the ground, then crossed to the dome. Winton and the Doctor followed, saying nothing. As they approached the door, two other colonists came out carrying a make-do stretcher. On it lay the body of Jane Leeson.

'We thought of taking them both to the main dome,' one of the men said to Ashe, partly as a question.

'Yes,' said Ashe. 'I suppose that's the right thing to do.' He turned to the Doctor rather shamefacedly. 'We never reckoned on people dying or being killed in the colony. We'll have to work out what to do.'

The three men waited until the stretcher had been carried out. Then they entered the little dome. The simple furniture had all been wrecked. 'We found her

41

over here,' said Winton, indicating the radio-telephone. 'He was outside, where you saw him.'

'How did you get here before us?' asked the Doctor.

'We were patrolling,' said Winton. 'We heard the thing.'

'Did you get a shot at it?' asked Ashe.

'Yes,' said Winton. 'All three of us blazed away like mad.'

'So you actually *saw* it?' the Doctor said.

'For a few moments,' said Winton. 'Like a big lizard it was, from the picture books.'

The Doctor found the last remark strange, then remembered that these people of the year 2972 had probably never seen any real animals. All the Earth animals had been systematically exterminated by Mankind by the year 2500.'

Ashe asked:

'Where did it go?'

'It vanished,' said Winton. 'Just vanished into the darkness.'

While Ashe and Winton discussed the possibility of finding blood tracks—assuming the monster had been hit —the Doctor examined what appeared to be claw marks in the wood of the smashed kitchen table. From a claw mark it is possible to estimate the size of the claw, and from the size of a claw, one can calculate the probable size of the animal.

'This monster,' said the Doctor to Winton, 'was about twenty feet high?'

'Feet?' said Winton, puzzled.

The Doctor had forgotten that Earth had completely converted to metric measurements a thousand years ago. 'About six metres high?' he repeated.

'That's right,' said Winton. Then, suspiciously, he added: 'How do you know?'

'The size of these claw marks,' said the Doctor. 'And you found Mrs. Leeson's body by the radio-telephone?'

Winton nodded.

42

'Then we have a rather strange problem,' said the Doctor, 'because how could a twenty foot high—I mean, six metres high—lizard come through that door?'

6

The Survivor

John Ashe felt that his whole world was starting to fall to pieces. It hadn't been easy finding a group of people who might mix well together in a colony. Of the many people who replied to his advertisements, he had turned down the majority because they were too young, or too old, or just didn't seem right in some way or other. After each interview Ashe had taken the decision whether to accept or reject the applicant. Then, of the many secondhand spaceships that he looked at, he had decided which to buy for the group. The others all had their own ideas on how much food to take, but finally it was left to Ashe to decide on the exact quantities. He was now tired of taking decisions, but he knew that if he showed his feelings to the others the whole colony would collapse. They expected him to lead, and he tried not to let them down.

Then came trouble on the journey, when the spaceship almost blew itself to pieces shortly after lift-off. With the help of Leeson and Winton, both good engineers in their own ways, Ashe solved that problem. The journey took longer than they expected, but once they had landed everyone was happy. Then they saw the Primitives, and some of the women were terrified. Some of the younger men, who had never possessed a gun before, wanted to shoot the Primitives. Ashe had restrained them, and explained that they could and must live in peace with these strange people. The first days of sowing seeds brought great excitement because none of them had ever done physical work before; on Earth machines did everything. But the excitement soon gave way to aching backs and calloused hands, and sheer tiredness. Ashe had explained that this was part of their new life, and that they would get used to it. Then the crops failed to grow. And now two of the colonists had been killed—by a monster six metres high who could somehow enter a door less than two metres high.

By the time the Leesons' bodies had been carried to the main dome, the first rays of their alien sun were shooting like fiery fingers into the eastern sky. All the colonists had come to the main dome, and now they all looked at Ashe and expected him to *do* something, to take another decision. When people died on Earth it was always in a hospital, and the hospital operatives sent the bodies to a crematorium. Ashe looked at the two bodies laid side by side on make-do stretchers in the main area of the big dome, each covered now in old sheets, and wondered what he ought to do. It was impossible to build a fire such as they had in the crematoria, because they could never find enough wood.

It was this stranger, the Doctor, who somehow saw into Ashe's troubled mind and came up to him and spoke very quietly: 'You'll have to bury them.'

Now Ashe remembered reading an old audiobook about burying dead people, back in the time when Earth still had open land. 'Yes,' he said, 'we must dig holes.'

'Graves,' said the Doctor, so quietly that no one else could hear.

'Yes,' said Ashe, 'graves.'

'I have already asked two of your men to start preparing them,' whispered the Doctor. 'You and I must be pall-bearers.'

Ashe didn't understand him at first. But the Doctor went to the end of one of the stretchers, and Ashe realised he was expected to go to the other end. Two of the other men present got the idea, and went to lift the other stretcher. The Doctor lifted, and Ashe lifted, and the sad little procession left the main dome. All the other colonists followed in silence.

As the Doctor led the way to where two other colonists with spades were waiting by freshly dug graves, he turned his head and spoke over his shoulder to Ashe. 'Tell your daughter to have tea or coffee or something ready for our return.'

Ashe was bewildered. 'Why?'

'I'll explain afterwards,' said the Doctor.

Ashe called his daughter over to him as he walked carrying the stretcher, and gave her the order. She, at least, never questioned him. From the corner of his eye he saw her hurrying back to the main dome.

At last they were beside the holes, which the Doctor called graves. Here Ashe was glad to let the Doctor take over. The Doctor had ropes ready, so that the two bodies could be lowered gently down into their respective graves.

'Thanks,' said Ashe, glad that someone knew what to do.

'Now we have a service,' said the Doctor. 'What religion were they?'

'Religion?' said Ashe, not understanding.

'You must stand here and say some nice things about them both,' said the Doctor, still in no more than a whisper. 'You must say that they did not die for nothing.'

'Why?' asked Ashe.

'Because,' said the Doctor, 'all these people standing here expect it. They don't *know* that they expect it, because they've never met death before, not on your computerised, sanitised Earth.'

Ashe looked at the colonists. They were all standing there, eyes to the ground, waiting for something. 'All right,' he told the Doctor. 'I'll try.' He cleared his throat. He was used to speaking to the whole group, but never before like this. 'We shall miss Jane and Eric Leeson. Jane was always kind, and kept her head when the spaceship nearly blew up. Eric was a hard worker, and never afraid of anything. Some of you may think that they died for nothing. But they didn't, not really . . . they died trying to make a better life, not only for themselves, but for all of us. We shall not forget them.'

46

He stopped and looked at the Doctor for approval. The Doctor nodded, picked up some of the dug out soil in his hand and dropped it into first one grave then the other. Then the Doctor walked off quietly towards the main dome. Almost involuntarily Ashe did the same, picking up a few grammes of the powdery soil, and scattering them onto the corpses within the graves. Then he, too, walked away. One by one the other colonists did the same, scattering the soil of their planet onto their dead friends.

．　　　　．　　　　．　　　　．　　　　．

Back at the main dome Mary, helped by Jo, had synthetic tea waiting for them all. Ashe found the Doctor already there, joking with Mary about something. Ashe went up to him.

'Thanks,' he said. 'But is this a time for jokes?'

The Doctor drew Ashe away from the two girls, now busy serving tea to the other colonists as they sadly trooped back inside. 'To live away from your Earth,' said the Doctor, 'you've got to learn more than how to sow seed and use a plough. With death, there has to be a time for tears, and then a time to rejoice in the continuation of life. Hence the tea.'

'How do you know all these things?' asked Ashe.

'You might say,' said the Doctor, 'that I'm something of an historian. Except that to me the past, the present, and the future are all one.'

'All one?' said Ashe. 'That's impossible!'

But there was no time to pursue their talk. Martin, the colonist who had first seen a monster, came up to them. He talked loudly so that all the others could hear. 'It's no good, Ashe. We've got to admit defeat! We've got to go back to Earth!'

Ashe said, 'We've invested a year of our lives into this planet. We've got the beginnings of a colony . . .'

Martin didn't want to listen, and cut in: 'We can't even support ourselves, and now two of us are dead.'

'I wonder if I might join in the discussion?' enquired the Doctor.

Now young Winton came forward, to support Martin. 'This has nothing to do with you, whoever you are!'

'The Doctor is our guest,' Ashe reminded them. 'Please let him speak.'

'All right,' said Martin. 'But make it short.'

'What I have to say is very simple,' said the Doctor. 'I've spent some time studying your crop records. I believe that growth is inhibited by some unnatural force. We must isolate it and overcome it.'

'What about the monsters?' asked one of the women colonists. 'Can we have children grow up in a place overrun with monsters?'

'For a start,' said the Doctor, 'we know it isn't overrun with them. Only two have been sighted—and for that matter, it may be the same one seen twice. Now are you going to run like children from terrors in the dark?'

This quietened the colonists for a moment. None of them wanted to admit to being afraid. Ashe took the opportunity to speak again : 'This colony is our only chance, friends. If we leave it, we'll have nothing. If we stay, we may have a chance.'

It was Mrs. Martin, who herself had been terrorised by the monsters, who spoke up for Ashe's attitude. 'I think he's right. We've put too much work into this place to leave it now.'

'You see,' said Ashe, spurred on by Mrs. Martin's support, 'there's a chance if we keep pulling together. What we've got to do is to organise patrols for all the domes. The Doctor will help us with the agricultural problems...'

Ashe's voice trailed off as he saw the man stagger in through the main entrance. He was only about twenty-five years old, but his sunken eyes and hungry face made him look fifty. His clothes were in tatters. As he entered the dome he stood there for one moment as though trying to say something, then fell forward to the ground. Mary and Jo were the first to reach the man's side. Ashe and the Doctor quickly followed with all the colonists crowding around. The Doctor gently turned the man over onto his back; Mary raised his head. Jo hurried away to get the man something to drink.

Ashe asked, 'Where are you from?'

The man opened his mouth, but he was too parched to speak. Jo brought one of the little cups of synthetic tea, and put it to the man's lips. As he drank greedily the Doctor asked Ashe, 'Isn't he one of your colonists?'

'No.' Ashe again spoke to the man, 'Can you understand me? Where are you from?'

'Colony,' the man said.

Now Winton also crouched by the man. 'There's another colony on this planet?'

The man tried to nod his head. 'I've been wandering . . . for weeks . . . hundred of kilometres . . . wandering.' He seemed ready to faint.

Winton shook the man roughly. 'The other colonists, your friends. Where are they?'

The man's eyes closed, then opened again suddenly, and stared straight up at Winton. 'A year of hunger . . . crops wouldn't grow . . . then the lizards.' He closed his eyes tight, and his weather-beaten hands clawed into the ground as some memory of terror swept through his mind. 'Giant lizards . . . so many of them . . . then the Primitives.'

'The other colonists in your group,' Winton insisted, again shaking the man, 'where are they?'

'All dead,' the man said. 'Every one of them . . . killed . . .'

7
The Robot

Ashe and the Doctor walked slowly back to the Leesons'
wrecked dome. The Doctor particularly wanted to see
the damage again in daylight; and Ashe wanted to talk
privately with the Doctor.

'What should I do?' asked Ashe.

'For the time being,' said the Doctor, 'try to keep an
open mind.'

'After what that man Norton said?' Ashe was refer-
ring to the survivor from the other colony. He had not
yet regained consciousness but they had found his name
on a letter in his pocket. 'There's no hope for us.'

'How do you think Man first made out on Earth?'
asked the Doctor. 'He had to fight sabre-toothed tigers,
rampaging mammoths, diseases of all sorts. He survived.'

'But how many died in the struggle?' said Ashe. 'In
the natural fight for survival, it's only a few who live
through it. I've got to think about the lives of human
beings, not a set of statistics.'

'Maybe I'll find out something here,' said the Doctor,
indicating the dome that they had now reached. 'Anyway, we shall see.'

Ashe remained outside, staring blindly at Leeson's
blood now dried on the rocky ground. The Doctor went
into the dome, but he found himself with company : two
Primitives were searching around among the wreckage.
When they saw the Doctor they both immediately turned
and drew long knives from their belts, raising them in
defiance. With their painted bodies and faces, and
bright yellow hair, they were a fearsome sight.

'I mean you no harm,' said the Doctor slowly and
distinctly, not expecting them to understand, but hoping

that the tone of his voice might put them at ease.

Then Ashe entered behind the Doctor. Immediately the Primitives lowered their knives. 'This is a friend,' said Ashe.

'Do they have a language of their own?' the Doctor asked.

'I've never heard them speak,' said Ashe. 'But they seem to understand what I say.' He spoke up loudly again, to address the Primitives. 'What have you taken?'

The Primitives didn't move.

Ashe held out his hand, palm up. 'Come on now, I know you've taken something. It's all right if I *give* you things, but you mustn't take them.'

One of the Primitives untied from his belt a leather pouch, opened it and brought out a domestic tin opener, which he put into Ashe's hand.

'Is that all?' said Ashe.

The other Primitive also had a pouch, and produced a hair brush for Ashe.

'More,' said Ashe.

The first Primitive dipped his six-fingered hand into his pouch again and produced a little packet of biscuits. He looked at the biscuits rather sadly, wetting his lips with his tongue as though enjoying the treat at least in his imagination, then made to put the packet into Ashe's hand. Ashe withdrew it. 'You can keep the food,' he said.

Both the Primitives bared their teeth and hissed loudly, a sign of pleasure.

'All right,' said Ashe, 'off with you now.'

The two Primitives raced out of the dome, still baring their teeth and hissing in ecstasy. Ashe watched after them, then turned back to the Doctor. 'I wonder how long they'll stay playful like that,' he said. 'Once they know we're beaten, they'll turn on us.'

'I don't think you really believe that,' said the Doctor. 'Anyway, you're not beaten yet.' The Doctor knelt down and started very carefully to re-examine the claw marks on the smashed kitchen table. Ashe watched him for a while.

'What do you hope to find there?' said Ashe.

'I don't know,' said the Doctor, 'until I've found it.'

'Well,' said Ashe, 'I'll leave you to it. I'll be at the main dome.'

Ashe went away, which was exactly what the Doctor wanted. He took a magnifying-glass from his pocket and inspected one claw mark in detail. The marks were too regular to be natural. The Doctor needed to put tiny scrapings of the clawed surface under a powerful miscroscope to learn more about the true nature of the claw: was it that of an animal, or something made to *look* like one? He did not wish to carry a whole section of the smashed kitchen table with him back to the microscope which he had in the TARDIS, so he decided to cut out a claw mark. He inserted the blade of a very sharp little knife deep into the wood just at the side of one, at such an angle that the tip of the blade went under the mark. Then he sliced down the wood, and now repeated the process on the other side of the claw mark. Now he cut across the wood at the top and bottom of the gouged out line, so that finally he was able to lift out a sliver of wood which contained the claw mark. This he put into a test-tube, also taken from his capacious jacket pockets. Then he froze rigid.

With an earsplitting crash a hole was smashed through the wall of the dome at the back. Through it marched a metal robot, with arms, legs and head like those of a man. It made straight for the Doctor, its metal hands waving about in search of its prey. The Doctor stepped backwards. He stumbled over wrecked furniture and fell back heavily, banging his head against the dome's metal wall. The robot turned, seemingly attracted by the sound of the Doctor's fall, then continued forward again crushing the remains of the kitchen table with its huge metal feet. Just as a metal hand made contact with the Doctor's face, the robot stopped dead, lifeless, like a mechanical statue.

'You can get up now.'

From his position on the floor the Doctor couldn't see

With an earsplitting crash a hole was smashed through the wall of the dome . . .

where the voice was coming from, but it was human and sounded fairly friendly. The Doctor struggled to his feet. A man had followed the robot into the dome, through the hole in the wall. He was a tough, hardbitten man, in his late thirties. He had on a sort of uniform jacket and matching tunic, basically black but piped with bright red. Across the left breast of the tunic was an oval of red piping, and inside that the letters IMC. In his hand was a very small remote-control unit, a little black box with buttons and a dial on it : obviously the control box for the robot.

'You ought to keep that thing under better control,' said the Doctor.

'Yes,' said the man. 'Sorry. It's only a Class Three Servo robot, not very bright.' He looked round the room. 'What happened?'

'Something,' said the Doctor, 'or someone attacked this place last night. May I ask who you are?'

'Caldwell's the name,' he said, indicating the initials on his tunic with a grin. 'Interplanetary Mining Corporation. We're doing a mineral survey. Is this your place?'

'No,' said the Doctor. 'It belonged to two colonists.'

'Colonists?' said Caldwell, with surprise. 'Earth Control told us this planet was uninhabited.'

'Then Earth Control,' said the Doctor, 'whatever that is, is wrong. Presumably you'll move on to another planet for your survey.'

'That's not up to me,' said Caldwell. 'They'll have to sort it out at Earth Control. According to our records this planet has been allocated for mining.' He grinned. 'Maybe you people chose the wrong planet ! It's awful easy, once you're out in Space !'

'I rather doubt it,' said the Doctor. 'Now if you'll excuse me I have some work to do . . .'

The Doctor moved to leave, but Caldwell stepped right in front of him, still grinning. 'Look, I'm on the way back to my spaceship. How about coming back there with me?'

'Why?'

'Just trying to be friendly,' said Caldwell. 'Is there anything wrong with a little hospitality? We could talk about who's made the big mistake—us or you.' Friendly as he seemed, Caldwell remained standing firmly between the Doctor and the door.

'I'm sorry,' said the Doctor, 'but I've got a great deal to do. And I really ought to tell the colonists that you've arrived here.'

'But they're going to know,' said Caldwell. 'There are no secrets between friends, and on a desolate place like this we've all *got* to be friends—or wouldn't you agree?'

As Caldwell spoke he touched one of the controls on the little black box. From behind him the Doctor could hear the robot move again, a manœuvre which brought it close to the Doctor's back.

'I suppose I could spare you a few minutes,' said the Doctor.

'Great,' said Caldwell, flashing his boyish grin again. He gripped the Doctor's arm in a friendly way, led the Doctor to the door, then took a last look round at the shattered furniture. 'Something certainly made a job of wrecking this place. Good thing no one was hurt.'

'The two colonists who lived here,' the Doctor said, 'were killed.'

Caldwell released his grip on the Doctor's arm. 'Two people—killed?'

The Doctor noticed how shocked Caldwell was with the news of the deaths, almost as though Caldwell might have known the people who died. 'That's right,' he said, 'a man and his wife.'

Caldwell passed his hand over his brow. The boyish grin had vanished—he seemed totally deflated by this news. 'Well,' he murmured after a few seconds, 'the invitation still stands to come and see my people. They'll be glad to meet you. I've got a buggy outside.' With that, Caldwell walked out of the dome, apparently leaving the Doctor free now to follow or to go his own way. Whereas before the Doctor hadn't wanted to go with Caldwell, feeling it to be his first duty to tell Ashe about the arrival of an IMC survey team, now he was desperately keen to stick with Caldwell and try to find out why the news of the colonists' deaths had had such a marked effect on the man.

The Doctor left the dome. Outside stood a small electrically-powered vehicle rather like a bicycle with four wheels. Mounted on the chassis were four simple seating places. Caldwell was already sitting on one of the front seats before the steering wheel. The Doctor got on the seat beside him. Caldwell was staring straight ahead of him, as though still shocked by the news of the colonists' deaths.

'What about your robot?' the Doctor asked.

'What's that?' Caldwell turned to the Doctor. 'Oh yes, Charlie. I nearly forgot Charlie.' He pressed buttons on the little remote-control box. Within a moment the robot came walking out of the dome, and obediently climbed up and took its place on one of the back seats.

'Right,' said Caldwell, 'let's go.'

Caldwell drove in silence, apparently finding his way through reading a small compass built into the centre of the steering wheel. The Doctor soon realised that they were heading where he and Jo had left the TARDIS. 'How far are we going?' he asked the now silent Caldwell. The man grunted a reply to the effect that they only had a few kilometres to drive, but he didn't say how many. He drove in a dead straight line, up little hills and down into valleys, then up again. Nor did he make any effort to steer round the smaller boulders: the wheels of the buggy were made to bounce over almost any obstacle not larger than themselves. Eventually, the buggy was rolling down to where the Doctor and Jo had arrived. The TARDIS was gone.

'Will you stop, please,' asked the Doctor.

'My friends'll want to meet you,' Caldwell said, driving on.

'Afterwards,' said the Doctor. 'But there's something I want to check right here.' He put so much insistence into his voice that Caldwell stopped the buggy. The

Doctor immediately dismounted and went to the spot where the TARDIS had materialised after its journey from Earth. He suspected the Time Lords were really in control when the TARDIS took off from UNIT Headquarters: had they now dematerialised the TARDIS, leaving both Jo and himself stranded on this desolate planet for ever?

'Hey', shouted Caldwell, 'if you're trying to run away, I can outpace you easily with the buggy!'

But the Doctor continued undeterred to the exact point where he had last seen the TARDIS. Caldwell started the buggy again, and turned it savagely to pursue the Doctor. But when Caldwell realised the Doctor wasn't running anywhere, but was simply studying a patch of ground, he slowed down the buggy and got off to join the Doctor.

'Not that I expected you to run away,' Caldwell said, with a suggestion of renewed friendship, of trying to make up for an understanding that he wasn't sure had ever existed, 'but . . . well, what are you staring at the ground for?'

'I left something here,' the Doctor said, 'some very valuable equipment.'

'Yes?' Caldwell looked around the area. 'How big was it? What did it look like?'

'It was like a police . . .' But the Doctor thought better of it; Caldwell would never understand. 'It's a tall blue box,'—something caught his eye a little way off—'and I've got a very good idea who's taken it!'

What caught his eye were drag marks in the dust—that and a few wisps of bright yellow hair on the ground. The Doctor hurried over to the marks, then looked up in the direction they were going. He could see now the trail of the dragged TARDIS stretching away in a dead straight line towards some hills a couple of miles across a flat plain.

'The Primitives,' he said to himself. 'Why should they want the TARDIS?'

'What's that?' said Caldwell, not understanding.

'I'm afraid I'll have to leave you,' said the Doctor, 'and find this missing equipment of mine.'

Caldwell, whose outward good spirits seemed to have returned, grabbed the Doctor's arm. He gave his most boyish grin. 'But we're going to miss you.' With his free hand, Caldwell operated the robot's remote-control. 'Charlie's not going to like it.'

The robot responded by carefully dismounting from the buggy. It lumbered across towards the Doctor, its metal hands groping in the air ahead of it.

'My grip's nice and friendly,' said Caldwell. 'But Charlie, sometimes he doesn't know his own strength.'

By now the robot had come up to the Doctor. Caldwell pressed another button, and a metal hand encircled the Doctor's other arm.

'Couldn't you spare the time to have morning coffee with us,' said Caldwell, 'if only to make Charlie happy?'

'Kindly tell this metal moron to take its hand off me,' said the Doctor.

'Metal moron?' said Caldwell. 'Charlie isn't going to like that kind of talk.'

Caldwell brought his thumb down hard onto another button on his hand-held control unit. The Doctor nerved himself to feel the robot's grip tighten and crush the bone of his arm. Instead, from what served as the robot's mouth the Doctor heard a crude recording of what he had just said.

'Kindly tell this metal moron to take its hand off me,' came from the mouth of the robot. This was followed by guffaws of metallic laughter, from somewhere within the robot's head.

Caldwell grinned at the Doctor's seeming surprise. 'You see—me and Charlie are just a couple of jokers.' He pressed another button, and the robot's hand came away from the Doctor's arm. 'Shall we get back in the buggy now,' he said, 'and all be friends?'

'All right,' said the Doctor. 'Since you insist.'

8

The Men from IMC

Captain Dent sat in his captain's chair in the control room of the Interplanetary Mining Corporation spaceship, his eyes on the monitor screen. As a television eye in the body of the spaceship slowly moved round the ship's circumference, it projected onto the monitor screen a panning picture of the planet's rocky, slightly undulating surface. Despite years of service with IMC, it still gave Dent a thrill to sit inside the comfort and protection of a ship and be able to see everything that was outside.

As he sat there, his hands moved from one to another of the controls. He knew each lever and knob by touch, and exactly how much power he could exert with each of them, energy measured not only in thrust of the spaceship's motors but also in the destructive force of the weapons every IMC ship carried. Sitting like that, in his special captain's chair, with his hands gently touching and stroking the controls, he was always reminded of the power of the Interplanetary Mining Corporation and his place within that organisation. When he was a child his father had told him, 'You've got to work hard at school and at university, and then you must get into one of the big corporations and stay there, and they'll look after you.' He had listened to his father's advice. He had never wanted to be like his uncle, a man who had changed jobs many times in his life and still had no real position in the world. From the beginning, Dent wanted to work up to a good job, and that meant getting into a really big corporation and staying there. He was lucky enough to join IMC at the age of 20, one of five successful applicants that term out of seventeen thousand. Immediately, he got a room of his own to live in, a rare privilege for any unmarried man on the overcrowded planet Earth. He was given six months' training on spaceship maintenance; he studied day and night and never took the elevator up to the sunshine or went for Walks or attended parties. He graduated with honours. It was then that they gave him his special IMC uniform, piped with red, and sent him as a crew member on his first mission with a survey ship looking for much-needed minerals on other planets. On his return to Earth he not only got his share of the crew's bonus, but also a note telling him to report to the IMC personnel manager's office.

'We like your work,' said the personnel manager, 'and we want to promote you to First Officer for your next trip. However, I see from your file that you're not married.'

'That is correct, sir,' said Dent.

The personnel manager smiled, a smile that reminded Dent of his own father. 'The Corporation likes its First Officers, and its Captains of course, to be married. It makes a man feel more secure. Got any one in mind?'

'No, sir,' said Dent. He had always remembered his father's advice that the big corporations much preferred to choose the wives and husbands for their employees, so he hadn't tried to find a wife.

'Then let IMC help you,' beamed the personnel manager. 'I'll just run the details from your file through the computer, and see who it matches up with, and we'll have a nice wife and home waiting for you when you get back from your next trip!'

Six months later Dent returned to Earth again, this time with a bigger bonus. In the envelope with the bonus statement was a key bearing an address tag. This was his new home. His wife was waiting for him, quite a pretty young woman with short hair dyed dull blue, as was the fashion that month. 'Are you my husband?' she said as he let himself in.

'I imagine I will be,' he answered, looking round his new home. It had *two* rooms, a shower, a lavatory, and a tiny kitchen. He was amazed at the influence wielded by IMC which could get him anywhere to live in as big as this.

'It's all fixed,' said the girl. 'IMC had our State records stapled together in the Automatic Personnel File, so we're already married.'

'That's fine,' Dent said, still looking about his new living quarters. 'What's that?' He pointed to a set of knobs and dials in the tiny kitchen.

The girl explained it was the infra-red cooker, and spent the next hour showing Dent all the gadgets in their home. Finally he asked, 'Do you know how much all this is going to cost me?'

'I worked it out,' said the girl. 'Even if they make you up to Captain in a year, with your earnings you'll pay off IMC for all this in about twenty years' time. But, of course, by then we'll have moved to somewhere bigger, and there'll be children, so I imagine you'll be paying back IMC for just about the rest of your life!'

She laughed. It was a very pretty laugh. And now, for the first time, Dent really noticed her in among all the other gadgets of his new home. Over the next few days of leave he found that the IMC match-making computer had done a good job, and that the two of them were going to be very happy together. Two years later they had their first child, then their second, and both children were now in a school owned and run by IMC solely for the children of IMC staff.

As Dent sat there, touching the controls of the IMC spaceship, he felt happy and secure in the fact that he was an IMC man, with an IMC wife, IMC children, with a beautiful *four* room IMC home. His present and his future were as secure as IMC, and IMC would go on for ever.

These pleasant thoughts were pushed from his mind by the arrival of First Officer Morgan, who came hurrying into the control room with a file in his hand. 'I've just got the first survey results from the computer, Captain,' he said, showing Dent the file. 'There's enough duralinium on this planet to build a million living units on Earth.'

'Excellent,' said Dent. He had trained his mind to switch instantly from one set of thoughts to another. All the personal memories were now switched off, and he was eagerly scanning his eyes down the set of figures on the computer print-out contained in the file.

Morgan said, 'I can't think how this planet ever got assigned for colonisation, can you, Captain?'

'Does it really matter?' said Dent, still eagerly reading the figures.

'Look,' said Morgan, 'Caldwell seems to have found a colonist for us.'

Dent looked up at the monitor. On it they could see Caldwell on the buggy driving straight towards them. Seated by Caldwell was a tall man with curly fair hair dressed in a knee-length black jacket and a frilly white shirt. The robot sat at the rear.

Morgan was amused. 'Why's he wearing fancy dress?'

'All colonists are eccentric,' said Dent, which was something he had once read in an IMC handbook on interplanetary sociology. 'Otherwise they wouldn't be colonists. They're drop-outs from society.'

By now the buggy had gone out of range of the outside television eye, so presumably it was too close in to the spaceship: it had probably stopped by the outside entrance, and its passengers would be in the process of dismounting.

Morgan asked, 'What are you going to say to this eccentric?'

'The usual story,' said Dent. 'We've only just arrived, and we are surprised and shocked to discover that the planet has been colonised.'

'Why couldn't we just blast them off the planet?' Morgan said. 'We've got the weapons.'

Dent closed the file and looked up at Morgan. 'Politics, dear boy. Earth Government is supposed to care for *all* its people, not only the interests of big business.' He smiled. 'We have to do things in a *legal* way.'

'I did everything the way you told me, sir,' said Morgan. 'But it seems such a long way to go about things.'

'Maybe,' said Dent. 'But the IMC way is best. You're young. You'll learn.' He heard Caldwell's heavy footsteps coming along the main connecting corridor and quickly put the survey file out of sight in case Caldwell had the colonist with him. But Caldwell entered alone, and very angry.

'I've just come across a colonist,' Caldwell exploded. 'He says two people were killed last night!' He swung round on Morgan : 'You're only supposed to scare them, Morgan, not slaughter them!'

Dent was also annoyed with this news, but for different reasons. 'Did you know about this, Morgan?'

'He must have known!' bellowed Caldwell.

'Let him answer,' Dent said. He turned back to Morgan, who looked scared of Caldwell's anger. 'Well?'

'It was an accident,' Morgan said, his face flushed with guilt. 'They found me and started shooting.'

'You acted very foolishly,' said Dent. 'You should not have let them see you.'

Caldwell returned to his attack on Dent. 'Is that all you can say? That Morgan was "foolish"?!'

Dent hated rows. During arguments people exposed what was really going on in their minds, and Dent never wanted other people to know what he was thinking. He said nothing for a moment, then retrieved the survey file from where he had put it out of sight. He opened the file under Caldwell's nose. 'Look at these figures, Caldwell. This planet's got enough duralinium to double IMC's profits next year. Your own bonus will be big enough to retire on.'

Caldwell stared at the report. Dent watched Caldwell's eyes as they sped from line to line of the figures. One of the many lessons Dent had learnt from the IMC Staff Management School, which he attended for six months before becoming a Captain, was that money overcomes most staff problems.

'You're sure this survey is correct?' Caldwell asked.

'The computer's never been wrong,' said Dent.

Caldwell drew a deep breath, a sign that he was seeing Dent's point of view. 'All right,' he said. 'But no more killings.'

Dent snapped shut the file. 'Agreed. Where is your colonist?'

'I left him in the crew room,' said Caldwell.

That was a mistake. Non-IMC people should never be left alone anywhere in an IMC spaceship. But Dent just said, 'Fine. I'll go and see him.' He put the file away again, left the control room and went down the connecting corridor to the crew room. The door was locked on the outside, and Dent was pleased to note that Caldwell had shown at least some sense. He turned the holding bolt, and quietly opened the door. The eccentric-looking man he had seen on the monitor with Caldwell was standing watching the screen of the crew's entertainment console which no doubt Caldwell had turned on for him. On the screen was an architect's drawing of high-rise living units on a floating island in the sea. A woman's voice came from the console, explaining the drawings. 'With every square metre of the Earth's land masses now covered with building complexes,' said the voice, 'scientists have turned to new means for providing accommodation for our ever-growing population. These floating islands, rising to three hundred storeys, will provide living space for five hundred million people . . .' The man, apparently aware that Dent was watching his back, switched off the console and turned round.

'Welcome on board,' said Dent, crossing to the man with his hand extended. 'My name's Captain Dent. It's a pleasure to meet you, Mr.—'

'Not Mister,' said the man. 'Just Doctor.'

They shook hands.

Dent said, 'I'm surprised and shocked to find colonists on this planet. It seems your people made some navigational error coming here. This planet's classified for mining. Still, IMC is always willing to help brave, adventurous people such as yourselves. So if there's any way we can help you to get on your way, just tell us how.'

'I think you're mistaken,' said the Doctor. 'This planet is classified for colonisation.'

Dent had no intention to pursue this argument, at least not now. He said, 'But it's such an awful place to live! And I understand it's infested with some hostile animal life.'

'I find that extremely puzzling,' said the Doctor.

Dent took a careful look at the Doctor. The man hadn't got the weather-beaten face and rough, calloused hands of the typical colonist, the type of people Dent had met on many other planets; not only that, but the man's clothes didn't look like a colonist's work clothes. Perhaps the man was some kind of interfering inspector from Earth Government. 'Puzzling?' said Dent. 'Why?'

'When giant dinosaurs lived on planet Earth,' said the Doctor, 'that planet was covered in lush, tropical vegetation which fed them. There is little vegetation here.'

'Maybe they're flesh eaters,' said Dent.

'Then what flesh do they eat,' asked the Doctor. 'I've seen no signs of other animals here.'

If there was one thing Dent hated it was people who could think and reason. It was that kind of person who always caused trouble. He dearly wanted to put a bullet through the Doctor as he stood there. Instead, he smiled. 'I don't understand all that stuff,' he said, pretending to be a simple, non-scientific man, 'but these creatures seem to exist and they're killers. Surely you and your fellow colonists don't want to spend your lives fighting monsters?'

'As it happens,' said the Doctor, 'I'm not a colonist, I'm merely a visitor here.'

'May I ask on what business?' said Dent.

'Certainly you may,' said the Doctor; 'my own. However, I'm very interested in what the colonists are trying to do. It's possible that these giant lizards can be found and destroyed, or at least deterred from harming the colonists.'

'Is that what the colonists think?' said Dent. This is really what he wanted to know.

'They expected difficulties when they came here,' said the Doctor. 'But with patience they will survive.'

Dent knew he was near to losing his temper. 'But they shouldn't be here at all! My corporation has been assigned the mineral rights. You know how Earth desperately needs minerals!'

'Earth's needs,' mused the Doctor, 'or your corporation's profits?'

'What's good for IMC is good for Earth,' said Dent rather smugly, realising that he was now blustering against the Doctor's calm. 'There are over a hundred thousand million people back on Earth, and they need all the minerals we can find!'

'What those people need,' said the Doctor, 'are new worlds to live on, like this one. Worlds where they can live like human beings again, instead of like battery hens.

'That's not my concern,' said Dent. 'Minerals are needed. It's my job to get them.'

'Even if that reduces this planet to a slag heap?' said the Doctor. 'Now if you'll excuse me, I have lost some important equipment. I must go and look for it.'

An idea was already forming in Dent's mind as to how he could get rid of the Doctor by way of an 'accident'. 'What sort of equipment?' Dent asked.

'It's rather difficult to explain,' said the Doctor. 'You might say it is a tall blue box.'

Dent pretended to lose interest in the Doctor's lost equipment. 'Well, at least I can arrange transport for you back to your colonist friends. Wait here, please.'

'This time,' said the Doctor, as Dent was closing the door, 'do you mind *not* locking me in?'

'It's normal security procedure,' said Dent, 'when non-IMC personnel are on board. You won't be locked in for long.' He closed the door, and turned the locking knob. He stood in the corridor for a moment, thinking. He knew he had conducted the interview badly and was not much of a credit to IMC. Then he reminded himself that normally he didn't have to contend with intelligent people like the Doctor. Once colonists had been scared by monsters, they were usually only too happy to accept IMC's help to move them on to another planet. This time it would be different, at least until he had disposed of the Doctor. He went back up the connecting corridor to the control room. Morgan was alone.

'Where's Caldwell?' Dent asked.

'He got called down by the motor room people, sir,' replied Morgan, 'some minor problem they've got.'

'Uh-huh.' Dent slumped down into his special captain's chair. 'This man he brought in, he isn't a colonist. I think he's some kind of scientist. He noticed the vegetation here doesn't fit in with the existence of monsters.'

'Could he be working for Earth Government,' said Morgan, 'checking up on us?'

'Maybe,' said Dent. 'Anyway, I want you to drive him back to the colonists' place.'

'If he's going to cause trouble,' said Morgan, 'why not keep him here?'

'No,' said Dent, 'there would be questions. When Caldwell found him, he was investigating the wrecked dome. Right?'

'Right,' said Morgan.

'So,' Dent continued, 'if his body were found in the wreck, it would be obvious that the monsters had gone back and killed him.'

Morgan got up. 'Leave it to me, sir.'

'He says he's lost some equipment,' said Dent. 'You offer to help him find it—you know, play him along. That'll give me time to get the robot over to the wrecked dome to meet him there.'

'Thank you, sir,' said Morgan. He was eager to go and had his hand on the door knob.

'One final point,' said Dent. 'Nothing must go wrong.'

'I'll make sure of that, sir,' said Morgan, turning the knob of the door. But Dent still had more to say.

'You should have told me last night about those two colonists being killed,' Dent went on. 'On this planet *I* represent IMC, and you must always tell the Corporation everything, even when you make a mistake.'

'Yes, sir,' said Morgan. 'Sorry, sir.'

'That's all right,' said Dent. 'Now get on your way. And make it look good!'

Morgan hurried away. Dent liked Morgan. Morgan was ambitious and totally unscrupulous. Dent felt you could always trust people like that.

9
The Spy

From the moment of his arrival at the colonists' main dome, IMC Second Officer Wilfred Norton had been treated as a Very Important Person. That's what he liked about playing the 'survivor' every time Captain Dent arrived at a new planet. In his heart he had wanted to become an actor, but his father and mother told him that he ought to get work with one of the big corporations. Now he had the comfort and security of working for one of the biggest, IMC, *and* he had the chance to do some very real-life acting.

After his dramatic entrance, when he said that he was the sole survivor from another colony, the colonists washed him, fed him, and gave him clean clothes to wear. And now he was being given a tour of inspection by this young fellow called Winton. There were many rooms and corridors in the main dome, and he was being shown a small room one side of which was packed with the colony's main electrical junction and fuses. Compared with gleaming equipment inside the IMC spaceship, this tangle of wires and switches looked like a mess that would shame a junkyard. A man was working on one of the switches, removing it from a rough make-do control panel; he was being 'helped' by a Primitive.

'This is our power supply junction-box,' said Winton. 'This is Holden, our electrician.' He turned to Holden. 'This is Wilf Norton.'

Holden shook hands with Norton. 'Yes, I remember you coming in. You must have had a rough time.'

Holden turned back to his work, but asked Norton

about how he had survived so long alone on the planet, and Norton gave in answer the story that he had rehearsed so well. As they talked Holden removed the switch, obviously broken, and was about to drop it on the floor, when the Primitive reached out for it.

'Sorry,' said Holden with a smile, 'that's for you.'

The Primitive took the discarded switch and quickly attached it to his belt which already carried various bits of broken machinery.

'What's he doing?' said Norton, indicating the Primitive.

'He's my assistant,' said Holden. As he spoke he reached out for a particular screwdriver on his little work bench; but the Primitive had already picked it up and was offering it to Holden. 'You see? He gets the right tool every time. Seems to know what's in my mind.' Holden started to use the screwdriver to install a newer switch.

'Our Primitives weren't that friendly,' said Norton. 'Where do you get your power from?'

Winton answered : 'We tap the old spaceship's nuclear generator and beam power through to the domes as they need it.' He turned to Holden. 'What's the trouble this time?'

'Same as before,' said Holden. 'All this stuff's had its time. Still, we soldier on.'

Norton followed Winton further down the corridor to the dome's dining area. The two girls, Mary and Jo, were cooking some stew. An idea was forming in Norton's mind, a plan that he wanted to carry out as quickly as possible. But first, while Winton still stayed with him, he had to talk to these two girls.

'That smells nice,' he said. 'What is it?'

'Only stew, I'm afraid,' said the girl called Mary.

'Whatever it is,' Norton said, 'I'm looking forward to it. For months I've lived on the roots of scrub.' He turned to Winton. 'I do appreciate the way you people are looking after me, and your showing me around the place. But if you want to get on with your work now,

I'll be all right.' He gave Winton a big wink which the girls didn't see, and nodded his head towards Mary.

Winton got the point. Norton hadn't spoken to a girl for months, and maybe he had taken a fancy to Mary. 'Well,' said Winton loudly, 'perhaps I should get on with some work. So, I'll see you later, Wilf.' With that Winton left the dining-hall.

'That really does smell good,' Norton said. 'About how long before you serve up?'

'Fifteen or twenty minutes,' Mary said.

'Then I'll go and wash my hands,' Norton said. He went to the door in to the corridor, then paused for effect. 'I'll never forget you people. Never in my whole life.' He looked at Mary and smiled, and she smiled back sympathetically and warmly. Then he turned and quickly went back towards the room containing the colony's make-do electrical power supply junction. The door was partly open, and he could see Holden inside just finishing his work connecting the new switch.

'There we are,' Holden was saying to the Primitive, 'that should hold for another few days. Put the tools away, will you? I just want to check the circuit relay.'

The Primitive began picking up the various tools that Holden had used: he carefully replaced each tool into its right place in a tool-box on the little work bench. Meanwhile Holden gave his attention to a fuse-box on the far wall, so that he had his back to the door.

Norton planned his every move before going in. From the corridor he could see a large spanner lying on a shelf between himself and the Primitive. The Primitive was sideways on to him at the moment, but any time now he would have to turn his back in order to pick up one of Holden's tools. Suddenly Norton realised how much it compared with an actor waiting to go on stage. There he was, standing in the wings, waiting for his cue. He could see the other actors already on stage, but he had to wait till exactly the right moment to make his entrance. He could see his most important 'prop', the big spanner that he must remember to pick up on entering. The only thing was an audience; but in the circumstances that was perhaps as well.

The Primitive turned his back to pick up the last tool. Norton entered silently, picked up the big spanner and raised it above his head, all in one movement. Just as the spanner was arcing down onto the back of the Primitive's head, by some telepathic means the victim sensed his danger. He ducked, and instinctively tried to grab his spear which stood against the wall. But he was too slow. Before his hand could reach the weapon, Norton had raised the spanner again and brought it crashing down upon the skull of the unfortunate Primitive.

Holden whirled round. 'What the—?' Then he saw the Primitive lying dead on the floor. 'You must be crazy!' he yelled at Norton. 'What do you think you're doing?'

Norton had found his audience—an audience of one startled man. Taking his time, he put down the big spanner, then picked up the spear. It was an actor's traditional joke that to be on stage carrying a spear means that you have only a very small part to play in the drama. And actors never had a chance to use their spears, not in real life.

'Put down that spear,' ordered Holden. 'What you've been through—it's affected your mind.'

Holden was standing well away, his back to the far wall.

Suddenly, Norton lunged straight at Holden with the spear, aiming for the heart. It found its mark. Then, seizing the big spanner again, he quickly smashed fuse-boxes, switch controls, and electrical junction-points.

Norton raced back to the dining hall. The colonists' leader, Ashe, was talking to Mary and Jo. 'Please,' he called out to Ashe with the strained voice of a man who had just seen murder done, 'you've got to come with me.'

'What's the matter?' Ashe asked.

'Come with me, *please*,' said Norton, grabbing Ashe's

72

Norton lunged straight at Holden with the spear, aiming for the heart . . .

arm and pulling him towards the corridor. 'It's terrible! It's murder!'

Ashe came running after Norton towards the electrical room, the two girls following. Norton stopped abruptly at the door to the room, covering his eyes, waiting for Ashe to catch up with him.

'What *are* you talking about?' Ashe demanded.

'Look,' said Norton, and pointed into the room.

Ashe looked, then spun round on Mary and Jo. 'No, keep back! I don't want *you* to see this.' He put his arm round Norton, who was now weeping. 'What happened?'

'I was coming by,' Norton said, between sobs. 'I saw it all . . . he didn't have a chance.'

'The Primitive killed Holden?' Ashe asked.

Norton nodded. 'He went for me, too, but I grabbed a

73

spanner and hit him. I know it was in self-defence, but I've never killed anyone or anything in my life before.' He continued to sob, his shoulders heaving.

'You couldn't help it,' said Ashe, as he glanced around the room. 'The relay circuits have been wrecked.'

'Holden must have caught the Primitive messing about with the controls,' said Norton, 'smashing things. That's why he got killed, with that awful spear.'

'Unless we get this lot repaired,' said Ashe, in his matter-of-fact way, 'the whole colony will come to a standstill. We can't go on without electricity. And Holden was the only electrician we had.' He left Norton, stepped into the room and looked down at Holden's body. 'Poor man, to die like this.'

Norton parted two of the fingers covering his eyes in order to watch Ashe as he stood over Holden's body. He congratulated himself on a marvellous performance.

10

The Claw

After Dent left the Doctor in the crew room, he did not again try the door: he knew it would be locked. To bide the time the Doctor again switched on the entertainment console. Flashing coloured lights swam onto the screen, and these were accompanied by a low thumping sound and occasional groans. He couldn't make out whether this was present-day symphonic or pop music, so he turned it off. Then he sat down, and took in the detail of the room. A ship this big, he reckoned, must have a fairly large crew, but this room had only four sleeping bunks. Obviously these were the officers' quarters: Caldwell had thought to put him in here so as to conceal from him the true extent of the spaceship's complement. He wondered where the crew was housed, and how many there really were. Then the door opened and a fresh-faced young man in IMC uniform stepped inside.

'First Officer Morgan, sir,' he said deferentially, 'at your service. Captain Dent asked me to drive you back to where you came from.'

The Doctor rose. 'That's very good of you. Perhaps you'd better lead the way.'

But Morgan stood to one side of the open door. 'No, sir,' he said, 'you're our guest. After you.'

'I suppose you're right,' said the Doctor, going into the connecting corridor. 'Just in case I take the silver.'

Morgan closed the crew room door and followed the Doctor. 'The what, sir?'

'An old fashioned joke,' said the Doctor.

'Oh, yes, sir,' said Morgan. 'Very amusing.'

The Doctor remembered his way out of the IMC

spaceship. The entrance, he noted, did not appear to be guarded. Outside was a buggy, similar to the one Caldwell had used to bring him here.

'Is this for us?' said the Doctor.

'Yes, sir,' said Morgan. 'Please take your seat.'

The Doctor sat by the driver's seat, and then Morgan took his position. Before starting, Morgan produced from his pocket a miniature two-way radio, pressed the transmitting button and spoke into the built-in microphone. *First Officer Morgan to control. Am taking guest to his venue, starting now.*

After a moment Dent's voice replied through the two-way radio. *Control to First Officer Morgan. Message received and understood. Carry on.*

Morgan pocketed the little two-way radio. He turned to the Doctor with a friendly smile. 'I understand from Captain Dent that you've lost something and want to look for it. With the buggy we could cover quite a distance, if you want.'

'That's very kind of you,' said the Doctor. 'Can you spare the time?'

'Strictly speaking,' said Morgan, 'each trip with the buggy has to be logged, and accounted for. But no one's going to notice a few kilometres here or there. Where do we start?'

The Doctor pointed. 'In that direction, I think.'

'Right,' said Morgan. He set the buggy in motion and steered the way indicated by the Doctor. 'What is it we're looking for?'

'A rather tall, blue box,' said the Doctor.

.   .   .   .   .

'With no trees or anything,' said Morgan as they drove along, 'every little thing shows up for kilometres on this planet. So it maybe it won't be too difficult to find.'

Within fifteen minutes they were at the flat plain where the Doctor had seen the drag marks leading from where the TARDIS had materialised. 'It was there,' said the Doctor, pointing, 'but you can see it's been dragged towards those hills.'

'Okay,' said Morgan, starting up the buggy again. 'This looks easier riding than those little switchback hills.' He drove ahead, following the dead straight line of the drag marks, but not very fast. After five minutes the hills seemed to be no nearer.

'Is this the maximum speed?' asked the Doctor.

'Well, no, sir,' said Morgan. 'But we're not in a hurry, are we?'

'Of course not,' said the Doctor.

They drove ahead for another few minutes. Then a bleeping sound came from the pocket where Morgan had put his little two-way radio. 'Excuse me, sir,' said Morgan, stopping the buggy and pulling out the little radio. He pressed the transmitting button. *'First Officer Morgan responding. What is your message?'* He listened, and they heard Dent's voice.

'Your buggy monitored on radar going away from, I repeat away from, colonists' dome,' Dent's voice said. *'What are you doing, First Officer Morgan?'*

Morgan looked at the Doctor, smiled and shrugged. *'Just trying to help our guest, Captain,'* he said. *'He wanted a ride.'*

Dent's voice replied: *'We are not in the joy-ride business, Morgan. Rectify immediately.'*

'Yes, sir,' said Morgan into the radio. *'Message understood.'* He returned the radio to his pocket. 'I'm sorry about that, sir, but we've got to go back.'

'I understand,' said the Doctor.

Morgan steered the buggy into a wide U-turn, then slowly headed back the way they had come. They passed the starting point of the drag marks, then mounted the first hill which the Doctor and Jo had climbed on their arrival on the planet, and slowly went down the other side. Morgan said, 'Doesn't this take us near where those poor people were killed?'

'It's in a straight line from here,' said the Doctor, 'just over another couple of hills.'

Morgan said nothing as they rode over the next two hills. Then the Leesons' dome was in the little valley before them. 'That the place?' asked Morgan. The Doctor nodded. 'I wouldn't mind taking a look at the damage those creatures caused,' said Morgan. 'Mind if we stop off for a minute?'

Morgan halted the buggy outside the little dome, dismounted and stood and stared at the front of the dome. The Doctor remained seated on the buggy. Morgan turned and asked, 'Where did they find them?'

'You can see blood stains over there,' said the Doctor, pointing. 'The woman was found inside.'

'Is it safe to go in?' asked Morgan.

'I imagine so,' said the Doctor who, filled with suspicion, was secretly very much on the alert, and was intrigued to see how Morgan was going to get him to get off the buggy and go into the dome. 'Why not take a look?'

'Won't you come with me?' asked Morgan. 'I'd like to know exactly what happened.'

The Doctor felt Morgan was just too pathetic to play with any more. He got down from the buggy. 'Certainly I'll come with you.' He strode into the dome, and Morgan followed. 'What is it you want to know?'

Morgan stood surveying the damage, in apparent awe. 'Where was the woman found?'

The Doctor pointed. 'There.'

Morgan inspected the wrecked kitchen table. 'These claw marks look fearsome.'

'Yes, indeed,' said the Doctor. 'It was all very efficiently done.'

'What do you mean?' said Morgan.

'I think the whole thing was faked,' said the Doctor, 'by someone who wants to frighten the colonists away.'

'You mean someone made these claw marks in the furniture?' asked Morgan, still pretending not to understand.

'Yes,' said the Doctor. 'With some mechanical device.'

Morgan took from another pocket a little control unit,

78

a replica of the one with which Caldwell had controlled the robot. 'You mean something like this?' he asked, and pressed one of the controls.

The robot entered through the hole in the wall, its arms extended forward towards the Doctor. But now the metal hands had been replaced by big metal claws. Morgan pressed another control, and the robot stopped. With his free hand, Morgan pulled a small handgun from his trouser pocket, then backed to the main entrance, cutting off the Doctor's escape.

'I wondered why we had all that charade about looking for my lost equipment,' said the Doctor. 'Of course your accomplices needed time to get the robot in position behind this dome.'

'That's right,' said Morgan. 'When Captain Dent radio'd me to say he'd picked us up on radar, that really meant Charlie was in position for the kill.' He paused, and licked his dry lips. 'I'm sorry about this, sir, really sorry. I hope you realise there's nothing personal.' He pressed a button on the remote-control, and immediately the robot's clawed arms started to flay, and then its legs began to move it towards the Doctor.

The Doctor jumped to one side, and the robot paused, its in-built sensories calculating where the Doctor had gone. 'It's not very quick on the turn,' remarked the Doctor, sidestepping again.

'It's slow but sure,' said Morgan, holding his gun on the Doctor. 'It always gets its man—or woman.'

The Doctor sidestepped again, and again the robot paused, then redirected itself towards its quarry. Now the Doctor was close to Morgan.

'There's no escape, I'm afraid,' said Morgan. 'Might as well give in gracefully. It'll be over in seconds.'

The Doctor made another move which brought him even closer to Morgan.

'Now keep away from the entrance,' warned Morgan, 'or I'll shoot!'

'If you shoot,' shouted the Doctor in reply, 'and my body's found with a bullet in it, that'll mess up your

79

Morgan found himself looking straight into the flaying claws of the robot—unable to break out of the Doctor's hold.

story about monsters!' And having said that, he suddenly dived for Morgan's gun, knocking it from his hand. Then he grabbed Morgan's left hand, the one holding the remote-control, and twisted it up behind the man's back.

'You'll break my arm!' Morgan screamed.

The Doctor wheeled Morgan round, to put him between himself and the oncoming robot. Morgan found himself looking straight into the flaying claws of the robot, and unable to break out of the Doctor's hold.

'It'll claw me to death!'

'Drop the remote-control,' shouted the Doctor in Morgan's ear. 'Drop it!'

Morgan screamed in agony as the tip of a claw drew a stripe of blood down one cheek. Almost involuntarily his hand released the remote-control. It fell to the ground, and its casing split open revealing a compact bundle of now exposed transistors and diodes. At the same time, the robot came to a complete halt; and then, after a second, it swayed and fell over backwards with a resounding crash.

The Doctor released his grip on Morgan's arm. Morgan stood there, gasping for breath. Then he made a dive for the gun on the floor. But he was too exhausted to move quickly enough: the Doctor kicked the gun away from Morgan's groping hand, and picked it up himself. Seeing this, Morgan turned and fled. He leapt onto the buggy outside and drove away at top speed.

The Doctor looked at the gun in his hand, then dropped it into his coat pocket, and sadly walked away from the dome.

11

Face-to-Face

The colonists' main dome came onto Dent's control room monitor screen in a bird's-eye-view. Using the IMC ship's powerful rocket drive, he had lifted the ship from its original landing place and now intended to bring it down next to the big dome. All his technicians were in their places in the control room, and above the low hum of the motors he could hear their chatter all around him :

'. . . Radar probe confirms terrain firm . . . main retro-rockets steady . . . descent rate now at minimum . . . landing stabilisers activated and in position . . . final altitude report . . . twenty metres, fifteen metres, ten, nine, eight, seven, six, five, four, three, two, one . . . we have contact !'

Dent remained in his captain's seat while the motors slowed and finally stopped. He intended to have a face-to-face meeting with the colonists, and to blockbuster them off the planet. By now, if Morgan had done his job properly, the Doctor would be a mangled corpse in the dome where the two colonists had died. Dent had had objections from Caldwell about killing the Doctor. At one point Caldwell seemed about to go after Morgan and the Doctor, in order to stop the former in his work. Dent had had to remind him that if he defied his (Dent's) ruling, he would be sacked from IMC, and put on a black list that would mean his never working again for any other mining corporation. Caldwell would lose his living unit on Earth, his income, and might end up sweeping the corridors of one of Earth's great building complexes. That, finally, persuaded Caldwell to back down.

One of the technicians said, 'All's clear, Captain. The

motors are dead. We've practically landed in the colonists' lap.'

Dent rose from his chair and put on his captain's helmet. Caldwell looked into the control room. 'You want me to go with you?'

'No,' said Dent firmly, 'I'll handle this.'

Dent went down the connecting corridor, and then for the first time stepped onto the terrain of the planet. The IMC ship had landed right in front of the colonists' main dome. A group of these poorly-clothed, hungry-looking people were standing watching from the entrance to the dome. Dent walked over to them.

'Captain Dent,' he said. 'IMC Survey.'

A young man stepped forward. 'You've no right to be on this planet!'

An older man restrained the younger one. 'All right, Winton, let me deal with this. My name's John Ashe. I'm the leader of this colony. We have been established for some considerable time and—'

Dent cut in: 'Can't we talk inside your dome?'

'I'm sorry,' said Ashe, 'yes, of course. This way.'

Dent was led into the main meeting area. All the colonists gathered round to hear the confrontation. Dent was glad to see First Officer Norton in amongst the colonists—at least *that* part of the scheme seemed to have worked.

'I can assure you, Mr. Ashe,' said Dent, 'that I'm as surprised as you are. As soon as we met your friend we realised that we must make contact with you people immediately, to sort things out.'

'What friend?' queried Ashe.

'He said he was visiting your colony,' said Dent. 'A tall man, who calls himself "the Doctor". Hasn't he returned yet and told you about our meeting? He insisted on setting off in advance of us.'

A pretty young woman spoke up from the crowd. 'Mr. Ashe, since the Doctor hasn't returned yet, couldn't you send out a search party? Something may have happened to him.'

'All right, Jo,' replied Ashe, 'all in good time.' He turned back to Dent. 'This planet has been assigned for colonisation.'

'Not according to us,' said Dent. 'We've been granted full mineral rights. We want to move in heavy mining equipment straight away.'

Norton took his cue to speak up. 'There's plenty of other parts of the planet you could mine! Why pick on here?'

'Our survey's been done here,' said Dent. 'We know for certain the minerals are in this part. In any case, we've been granted mineral rights for the whole planet.'

'I have a photostat copy of the certificate,' said Ashe, 'proving that this planet is for colonisation only.'

'I have a copy of a certificate,' retorted Dent, 'proving the opposite.' He didn't really, but he knew he could produce one pretty quickly once back in the IMC spaceship. 'There's only one solution to this,' he went on, 'we'll have to send for an Adjudicator.' He referred to the special Earth Government officials whose job it was to sort out claims and counter-claims.

Winton pushed his way to the front again. 'You know it can take months, years even, for an Adjudicator's decision, and by then you'll have gutted the planet!'

Dent ignored this. He spoke again to Ashe: 'I'm sure you agree that we must apply the proper procedures?'

Ashe was clearly swayed by what Winton had said, but he nodded and replied, 'Well, I suppose so.'

'Good,' said Dent. 'I'll use my ship's radio to ask Earth to send someone.' He turned on his heel to leave, and found himself facing the Doctor who had just entered.

'Sorry to still be alive,' said the Doctor to Dent. 'It must seriously upset your plans.' The Doctor turned and addressed himself to the whole gathering. 'This man tried to have me killed. They're trying to frighten you away with imaginary monsters that don't really exist.'

By now Dent had partly recovered himself. 'That's a very serious allegation, Doctor.'

'I know,' said the Doctor, 'and its one that I shall have

pleasure in making to the proper authorities. I imagine this Adjudicator will be very interested in your activities, Captain Dent.'

Dent turned back to Ashe. 'When I first saw your friend I thought he was eccentric. Now I'm convinced he's mad. I'll send a message to the Adjudicators' Bureau immediately. Excuse me.' And with that, Dent left the dome as quickly as possible. He had never been so humiliated in his life, and he was seething to get his hands on First Officer Morgan.

He found Morgan in the ship's crew room, drinking astrobeer. Overwhelmed with a rage, which he now did nothing to conceal, Dent knocked the astrobeer can from Morgan's hand and then hit him across the face. Morgan fell to his knees.

Dent kicked him and roared, 'Get up!'

Morgan slowly got to his feet. He touched his bruised cheek. 'You've no right to hit a member of the staff,' he cried, 'It's against the rules!'

Dent hit out again, and again Morgan fell to his knees. 'I'm doing this,' he said, 'instead of killing you. What happened?'

This time Morgan remained where he was, crouching on the floor. 'He smashed the robot's remote-control unit. He could have killed me!'

The door opened and Caldwell entered. When he saw Morgan grovelling on the floor in front of Dent he grinned and said, 'So, have you got the crew praying to you now, Captain?'

'Morgan has failed again,' said Dent, and briefly explained how the Doctor had walked in on his meeting with the colonists.

Caldwell listened, more amused than upset. 'I'm glad I'm only the mining engineer, and not one of you executives. Are you going to send for an Adjudicator?'

'Of course,' said Dent. 'Legality must always be maintained.'

'Meaning,' said Caldwell, 'that IMC will bribe the Adjudicator to give the right decision?'

85

'That remark,' said Dent, who had now thoroughly lost his self-possession, 'is slander! IMC *always* keeps to the law!' He knew this was totally untrue, but it was what he had been taught to say. 'I should put you both on a charge of insubordination!' The tiny two-way radio in his tunic pocket started to bleep. He pulled it out viciously, and snapped '*Yes?*' into its tiny microphone.

The voice was almost inaudible. '*Captain Dent?*'

'*Who's speaking?*' Dent shouted at the two-way radio. He held it close to his ear to hear the answer.

'*Norton here,*' said the whisper of a voice, '*from the colonists' main dome. Two colonists are just about to enter the ship.*'

Dent's temper faded away instantly. '*What for?*' he asked excitedly.

'*It's the girl called Jo and a young man called Winton,*' continued Norton's voice. '*They're going to look for evidence against us. They want to find out about the monsters.*' The voice paused. '*Must go now,*' Norton said. '*Someone's coming . . . don't want to be caught.*' Norton went off the air.

Dent went into action. 'You two stay in here.'

'Why?' said Caldwell.

'For once obey an order without asking questions,' Dent said icily. 'And keep the door locked from the inside.' He left them and hurried into the connecting corridor, and thence to the control room.

A number of his technicians were there. He grabbed the microphone next to his captain's seat. '*Now hear this,*' he said, addressing everyone on the ship. '*We have visitors. I want them to be let in—so no guards at the entrance to the ship. Lock all doors to rooms. Leave the connecting corridors free of personnel. Do not, I repeat do not, interfere with our guests in any way.*' He then told the technicians in the control room to conceal themselves wherever they could—behind chairs, under the main console, behind the door. Then he waited. Five minutes later the door to the control room opened slowly and Jo looked inside.

'The whole ship's deserted,' she said, and came on in. Winton followed her.

'Where should we look for evidence?' Winton asked.

'I don't know,' said Jo. 'Maybe in here.'

Dent stood up from where he had been crouching behind his captain's chair. He held a gun in his hand. 'Is there anything I can do to help you?' he asked.

12

The Bomb

Jo turned to escape, but suddenly the control room of the IMC spaceship was full of IMC men who had been hiding. She and Winton had walked into a trap.

'Grab them,' ordered Dent, and the IMC men pinned the prisoners' arms behind their backs. 'Now let me explain our mining methods,' said Dent. 'We use a lot of explosive charges—bombs, if you like. These bombs are exploded by remote-control radio. A charge set ten or twenty kilometres from here can be made to explode by a touch of this button.' Dent put a finger on to a button on the control console. He turned to Jo. 'Your friend the Doctor will be invited here. I shall explain that if he does not retract his ridiculous story about attempted murder, I shall press this button. I shall also explain that you and your companion will be killed instantly if I am moved to press that button.' He then turned to his men. 'All right, carry out the exercise.'

The IMC men set to work binding their prisoners' arms and legs, and gagging them. Then big plastic sacks were brought in, and Jo and Winton each put into one. After that Jo was conscious of being carried down a corridor, into the open, and then being driven on some vehicle for a distance over the rough terrain. When the sacks were removed they were by the ruin of a small single-room stone building. It had no roof or door or windows. They were still surrounded by IMC men, who quickly removed the gags and untied their arms and legs. Then they were frog-marched into the ruin. Two IMC men inside were gently putting a plain metal box down in the middle of what had been the floor. A third IMC man was using a sledge-hammer to drive into the floor a metal spike with a big ring in it. Now an IMC man quickly put a manacle on to one of Jo's wrists, and another manacle on to one of Winton's, then attached chains from them to a ring on the plain metal box; and, having done that, he attached another chain from the box to the metal spike driven into the floor. The attachment of Jo and Winton to the metal box—obviously a bomb of some sort—and of the box to the spike in the floor was done in under a minute, and without a word being spoken by the IMC men. The job done, the IMC men stepped back, and the one who seemed to be in charge came forward and adjusted a control on the side of the box. Immediately, a light started to flash on top of the box. Under the IMC badge on this man's tunic was his name and rank in small letters: 'Security Guard Allen'. Winton wrenched wildly at his manacles, tautening the chain that held him to the metal box.

'I wouldn't do that,' cautioned Allen, 'unless you want to blow yourself to bits. In fact, I wouldn't move at all.'

'You're nothing more than criminals,' Jo shouted.

'We obey our orders,' said Allen. 'There can't be anything wrong in obeying orders.'

With that, the IMC men hurried away. Jo looked about herself. 'What is this place?'

'Primitive ruins,' said Winton. 'They must have built these little one-room houses at some time, but they don't now. You find these ruins all over the place.' He stared at the manacle on his wrist. 'What do we do now?'

'Try to get away, of course,' said Jo. Jo compressed her hand, folding in the thumb over the palm to see if she could gently pull her hand through the manacle without upsetting the explosive charge.

·   ·   ·   ·   ·

The Doctor returned grim-faced from the IMC spaceship. While he had been completing repairs to the colonists' electrical room, the message had come from Dent saying that Jo was in the IMC spaceship and wanted to see the Doctor. The Doctor went there immediately, only to be told by Dent that Jo was attached to an explosive charge at a hidden location, and that she and Winton would be killed instantly if the Doctor made any more trouble for IMC. He went straight to Ashe and reported what Dent had said.

'This is abominable,' said Ashe. 'Even if Jo and Winton committed trespass by entering the IMC spaceship uninvited, they should not be treated like this! I'll go and talk to Dent straight away.'

'I don't think you have grasped the position,' said the Doctor. 'These people have no interest in law and order, or fair play. If you go, Dent may kill his prisoners there and then.'

'What do you suggest?' asked Ashe. He was clearly at the end of his tether, only too willing for anyone else to take the decisions now.

'He said they were "somewhere",' said the Doctor. 'Maybe we can find them both.'

'I'll organise a search party immediately,' said Ashe.

'Not immediately,' the Doctor said, restraining Ashe. 'The IMC ship is on our doorstep. They can see everything we do. If Dent sees signs of a search, he'll press that button. We'll have to wait until after dark. The problem is—where has he put them both with the bomb?'

     •   •   •   •   •

Jo sat back, her hand bruised and the manacle still on her wrist.

'Why not give up?' advised Winton. 'If you jerk that box you could blow us sky high.'

Jo looked at the box. Its light was still flashing regularly. The thought crossed her mind that she had no idea whether the box really contained an explosive charge. Still, she thought it best to treat the box with great respect. One sudden jerk on the chain connecting the box to their manacles and it might blow up. Then she noticed the grease on the box; it ran in a long blob down one side and might have been some kind of packing grease. She reached forward to get some of the thick grease on to her fingers.

'Be careful!' said Winton. 'Don't touch that thing!'

'I *am* being careful,' she said, and rubbed the grease all over her trapped hand. With her free hand she gripped the manacle, only to realise that the grease on the fingers of her free hand wouldn't allow her to get a good hold on the manacle. 'You try,' she said to Winton. 'Keep your fingers away from any grease, get a good grip of my manacle, then pull!'

'I don't want to hurt you,' he said.

'And I don't want to freeze to death in this place tonight,' she said. 'Now do as I ask you.'

Winton crawled over to Jo and got a firm grip on the outside of her manacle. He pulled. Nothing happened.

'Put one foot into my armpit,' she said. 'Then you'll have something to pull against.'

'I might pull your arm out of its socket,' he said.

'Will you please do as I ask?' Jo pleaded.

Winton worked his way round so that he could put one foot under her armpit. Then he pulled on the manacle. Jo tried not to show the pain of having her arm pulled, in case any reaction from her might deter Winton. Little by little the manacle came down over her folded hand until she could feel the bones being crushed together. 'Keep pulling,' she said, holding back tears of pain. All at once the manacle slid over the knuckles, and her hand was free. 'Thanks,' she said.

'You'd better run for it,' Winton said. 'Find your way back to the main dome and tell Ashe.'

'Not without you,' she replied. 'If the grease worked for me, it can work for you.' She reached forward to get grease to put on to Winton's still manacled hand.

'My hands are much bigger than yours,' he said, holding up the fettered hand.

She looked. It was true. His hand could never slip

through the manacle. 'Then I must break the chain,' she said and started to hunt around for a couple of rocks of the right shape and size.

'Far better you get on your way,' he said.

But Jo had found what she wanted. She placed one rock under the chain to Winton's manacle, then used the other as a hammer. The chain showed no signs of damage, so she bashed harder and harder with her make-shift 'hammer'. Suddenly, the chain slipped off the rock she was using as an anvil. For a moment the suddenly-taut chain pulled at the box, and the box moved slightly. They both looked at it in horror. The light on the box started to flash at high speed, as though it were transmitting some warning.

.   .   .   .   .

In the IMC ship's control room, a light on the main control console flashed on and off at short intervals. Morgan was the first to notice it. 'Captain,' he said, 'something's happening with that explosive charge.'

Dent grabbed his console microphone. *'This is Captain Dent to Security Guard Allen. Notify location.'*

Nothing for a few moments; then Allen's voice from the loudspeaker. *'On the way back to the ship, Captain.'*

Dent said, *'Go and re-check your prisoners immediately.'*

Allen's voice replied, *'Message understood.'*

.   .   .   .   .

Jo looked with delight at the broken links of Winton's manacle chain. Winton was already on his feet. 'Come on,' he said, 'let's go.'

They ran out of the ruined little house, then stopped. 'Which way?' said Jo.

Winton looked up at the sun. 'I reckon that way,' he said, and pointed.

They started running. As they began to climb a small hill of rock and scrub, the IMC four-wheel buggy came over the crest of the hill. At the wheel was Security Guard Allen. He turned the buggy to come straight at Jo and Winton.

'Split,' said Jo, and immediately darted away from Winton, so that Allen would not be able to catch them both.

Allen turned the buggy to head straight for Jo. She sidestepped the machine, then fell heavily on to the rocks. Allen stopped and dismounted, and by the time Jo was on her feet Allen had his arm round her. With his free hand he pulled his gun. Winton had paused some little distance away, not knowing what to do.

'Keep running,' Jo shouted. 'Go and tell them where I am and what's happened!'

Winton turned and began running away. Allen took aim with his gun and fired. But the shot missed. In a moment Winton was over the crest of the hill.

Allen pocketed his gun, and pulled out his little two-way radio. '*Security Guard Allen to Captain Dent,*' he said into the radio. '*Male prisoner has escaped, but have recaptured female.*'

Jo wriggled in Allen's grip, but the arm now round her waist was like a steel vice. After a moment Dent's voice replied over the little radio. '*Captain Dent to Security Guard Allen. Re-attach female to explosive charge, and from now on stay where you can see her. If I intend to activate the explosive, I shall give you ample warning.*'

'*What about the escaped male?*' Allen asked.

'*Other guards will be sent to pursue,*' said Dent's voice, '*and he need not be brought in alive . . .*'

. . . . . .

Winton stood gasping for breath at the top of another of the little hills. The position of the sun told him which direction to go to get back to the colony. He fingered

93

the bullet graze that ran along one shoulder. There was some blood, but it wasn't serious. His heart had stopped pounding now, and he started to jog-trot down the slope. Then he saw an IMC buggy coming over the crest of another hill. It wasn't Security Guard Allen this time : it carried four men in IMC uniforms, and they carried long guns. They spotted Winton almost instantly, and the buggy started to come towards him.

He stopped, and looked about him. There was no hiding-place, only open dusty ground and the little hills. For a moment he thought of giving in to them. He was tired and exhausted and the wound was beginning to hurt. All they'd do was take him prisoner again. He turned back to look at the buggy, with the half-formed idea of raising his hands in surrender. To his surprise, the buggy had stopped. Two of the guards were aiming their long guns at him. They both fired at the same time, and Winton heard bullets whistle past him and hit the ground beyond. These men had no intention of taking him prisoner : they were there to hunt him down and kill him.

In panic he ran away from the buggy, then suddenly realised he was making for a sharp incline of craggy rocks that the buggy couldn't possibly climb. Two more bullets were fired. One hit the rock ahead of him, and the other ripped through the trousers of his old workdenims. Now he started to dart from side to side as he climbed the steep embankment of rocks, thus presenting the IMC men with a more difficult target. As he climbed higher and higher, he looked over his shoulder to see what the IMC men were doing now. The driver had brought the buggy to the foot of the rocky steep, and now three of the IMC men were climbing after him.

But Winton was already well ahead now. He reached the top of the incline, raced over its crest, and then stopped dead when he saw what lay in the valley now below him. Next to a big plastic tent carrying the letters 'IMC' was a mechanical robot using a drill in the ground. An IMC man emerged from the tent and stood watching the work of the robot, but hadn't yet seen Winton. Winton calculated that on this downward slope he might be able to flash past the tent and the IMC man before the latter knew what had happened. Winton started running downhill at full speed.

The three IMC security guards found the rocky slope hard going. They weren't used to this kind of physical activity, and their uniforms restricted them. But they pressed on as best they could because they all had IMC living units back on Earth that they didn't want to lose, and IMC wives, and their children were in IMC schools that were very exclusive, and if they got the duralinium from this planet they would all get good IMC bonuses. Above all, they hated all colonists because they were eccentric and didn't conform to the society on Earth, and sometimes they smelt of sweat.

As the three IMC men reached the crest of the hill they heard two shots ring out. By the sound of the shots they knew they had come from one of the specially-made IMC handguns. Curious, they ran over the crest of the hill until they saw below them Caldwell's IMC tent, the robot, and Winton's body sprawled on the dusty hillside. Caldwell stood over the body, gun in hand. He looked up the hill.

'I got him for you,' he shouted up to them. 'Don't worry. Charlie here will dig a grave.'

The three IMC men turned back, to go down the rocky side of the hill again to their waiting buggy. One of them brought out his little-two-way radio and reported the success of the mission to Captain Dent, who seemed very pleased.

Outside the IMC tent, Caldwell remained exactly where the three security guards had seen him. When they were well out of sight he pocketed his gun and sauntered over to where Winton was sprawled on the ground.

'It's all right,' he said, 'they've gone.'

Winton slowly got to his feet. 'Thanks.'

Caldwell had gone into the tent, and gestured for Winton to follow. Inside there was a collapsible work

'See those silver-coloured veins in this rock?' said Caldwell. 'That's pure duralinium.'

table, and on its surface were various samples of rock which the robot had drilled out of the ground. Caldwell opened a first-aid box, took from it some antiseptic and started to clean up Winton's shoulder wound.

Winton said, 'Why are you helping me?'

'I'm a miner,' said Caldwell, 'not one of Dent's killers.' He took hold of a dressing and put it on Winton's shoulder. 'Listen friend,' he said, 'go back to your colony and persuade your friends to get off this planet.'

'We're waiting for the Adjudicator,' said Winton.

Caldwell picked up one of the rocks from the table. 'See those silver-coloured veins in this rock? That's pure duralinium. This is the biggest strike we've ever made. IMC want this planet, and they're going to get it.'

'But an Adjudicator's decision is law,' Winton protested. 'If he says we can stay, then it's all right.'

96

Caldwell stood back and grinned, but it was not a happy grin. 'I've just saved your life, young man,' he said, 'so that gives me the right to give you a little fatherly advice. Adjudicators can be fixed, understand?' He rubbed his fingers against his thumb. 'Money,' he said, 'that's all that really matters. I don't like it, and you don't like it, but that's how things work. So just you set about persuading your good people to get off this planet before anyone else gets killed.'

13

The Attack

Ashe called together the search party of a dozen men in the main meeting-room of the big dome. The Doctor explained to the men exactly what had happened—how he had been called back to the IMC spaceship where Dent had told him that Jo and Winton were chained to a bomb. When the Doctor had finished, Ashe spoke to the men.

'There are only two things we can do,' said Ashe. 'We can let ourselves be blackmailed by IMC, or we can go out and search for the prisoners.'

The response from the men made it quite clear that they were in no mood to give in to IMC.

'Fine,' said Ashe. 'With the IMC spaceship sitting on our doorstep, we'll have to wait till its dark before we leave.'

Norton spoke up. 'The prisoners could be anywhere. How do you expect to find them after dark?'

'There aren't many places to hide,' Ashe said. He went to a wall-map and pointed. 'There are some caves here, some Primitive ruins here and there, and that's about all.'

'But aren't we wasting our time with this proposal,' asked Norton. He pointed at the Doctor. 'We've only got *his* word about all this!'

'Why should I lie?' asked the Doctor.

Norton had his answer ready. 'Maybe you're really working for IMC. This is a trick to get all the men to leave the main dome so that the IMC men can walk in and take over!'

And at this point Winton staggered in clutching his wounded shoulder. He slumped down onto a chair and immediately told his story about the way in which he escaped from the bomb. Because of his state of exhaustion, the wall-map was taken down and brought over to him so that he could point to the ruins where he and Jo had been chained to the explosive charge. 'But your wasting your time going there,' said Winton. 'My guess is they'll have moved her somewhere else by now.'

'Why should they?' said Ashe, 'if they think you are dead?'

Winton didn't answer the logic of that. He rushed on to his next point instead. 'I've got a better idea. We'll take over their spaceship and send them packing!'

There was a murmur of approval from the colonists. But Ashe spoke up against the idea. 'We're not going to start a war, Winton.'

Winton looked up at Ashe. 'Look, I've been chained to a bomb, hunted, and shot at. As far as I'm concerned, the war's already started!'

'We must wait for the Adjudicator,' said Ashe.

'Remember what that IMC miner told me—the Adjudicator will be fixed,' said Winton. He went on, 'We'll take over their spaceship, make them release Jo, and send them back to Earth.'

'I absolutely forbid it,' said Ashe.

Winton summoned up the strength to struggle to his feet. 'We've listened to you for long enough, Ashe.'

'I'm the elected leader of this colony,' Ashe said. 'It says in our Constitution, to which you agreed, that although we run the colony on democratic lines, in a state of emergency the leader has the authority to act as he thinks best.'

'Then my best is better than your best,' retorted Winton. He turned his back on Ashe and said to the onlooking colonists: 'We'll attack in force in the morning!'

The male colonists gathered round Winton, to discuss the attack. Ashe found himself pushed out of the way. He turned to the Doctor. 'What can I do?'

The Doctor pushed his way through the crowd of colonists to Winton. 'You said one of the IMC men helped you. Where can he be found?'

Winton said, 'His name's Caldwell. He's got a tent pitched in the north sector.'

The Doctor looked at the map to check what was meant by the 'north sector', then quickly hurried out into the oncoming night.

.   .   .   .   .

The Doctor found Caldwell in the IMC tent. He was testing rock samples, using an instrument about the size of a fountain-pen that bleeped furiously every time it was pointed at a duralinium vein.

'Working out your future bonuses?' asked the Doctor from the doorway to the tent.

Caldwell looked up, surprised. 'Sort of. What do you want?'

'Your help,' said the Doctor.

Caldwell turned back to his work. 'I'm an IMC man,' he said quietly.

'Do you know that Captain Dent has got my companion, Jo Grant, chained to a bomb?' said the Doctor.

'That's just to scare you into keeping quiet,' said Caldwell. He went on working, or pretending to work. To the Doctor it was obvious that Caldwell's conscience was bothering him.

'Tomorrow morning,' said the Doctor, 'the colonists are going to attack your spaceship. I believe that might provoke Captain Dent to press the button.'

Now Caldwell stopped working and looked up. 'If those idiots attack the IMC ship,' he said, 'the guards will mow them down. You'd better stop that attack before it happens.'

'I don't know that I can,' said the Doctor, 'although I'm going to try. But there's something you can do.'

'What?' asked Caldwell.

'Release Jo,' said the Doctor, 'before the attack starts.'

Caldwell looked from the Doctor back to the bits of precious rock. He stared at the rock samples for some time. Then he drew a long breath. 'Why do you have to pick on me?' he said, still staring at the lumps of rock.

'Because,' said the Doctor, 'I believe that at heart you're really a good man.'

Caldwell continued to look at the rocks on the table top. Then, finally, he said : 'I'll do what I can. But you'd better stop that attack, Doctor. It won't be a battle. It'll be a slaughter.'

The Doctor left Caldwell staring at the rock samples.

.   .   .   .   .

An hour later saw Caldwell back in the control room of the spaceship. Morgan had just received news on the radio that an Adjudicator was on the way and would arrive soon. Dent was about to send another IMC guard to the Primitive ruin to relieve Security Guard Allen who was still keeping an eye on Jo.

'Don't bother about relieving the guard,' Caldwell said. 'Just have the girl brought back here.'

Captain Dent was taken aback by Caldwell's remark. 'What do you mean?' he asked.

'I've gone along with you in a whole lot of things,' said Caldwell. 'But chaining a girl to a bomb, that's pretty low! I want her brought back here immediately.'

Now Dent knew that Caldwell was serious. Had the man gone out of his mind? 'She stays where she is,' said Dent. 'And in case you've forgotten, I'm in command,' he added icily.

'And in case *you've* forgotten,' said Caldwell evenly, 'I'm your mineralogical expert. Either the girl's brought back, or the survey stops.'

Captain Dent had never met with insubordination like this before. He tried to remember what he had learnt during his staff management training. 'Caldwell,' he said, putting on a smile, 'we're sitting on the biggest duralinium strike in the history of IMC! This is no time for two old buddies to fall out about some stupid girl!' This was from page 44 of the Corporation's staff management handbook.

'We aren't buddies,' said Caldwell, 'and never have been. Bring the girl back, or I'm on strike.'

To strike was expressly forbidden by the IMC Terms of Employment, but Dent thought it best not to mention that. He tried another ploy. 'If you fall out with IMC,' said Dent, keeping up his smile, 'you've got an awful lot to lose. Your wife isn't going to like it if you don't have that nice IMC living unit back on Earth.'

'There's something the great IMC staff index doesn't know about me,' said Caldwell. 'My wife walked out on me just before this trip, so you can't use that on me any more. Bring the girl back, and you can keep my share of the bonus if you like.'

Dent held down his rising temper, and turned to Morgan. 'Have her brought back.'

Morgan just stared.

'Did you hear me?' Dent barked.

Morgan jumped to his feet. 'Yes sir. Right away, sir.' He hurried out of the control room.

Dent turned back to Caldwell. 'I don't know what game you're playing, Caldwell, but I hope you realise that you have just committed professional suicide.'

•   •   •   •   •

Jo felt her arm being tugged. She opened her eyes, saw Security Guard Allen looking down at her. 'Wake up,' he said. 'You're going back to the spaceship.'

She sat up stiffly, and saw that she was now manacled by both wrists to the bomb. Its light was no longer flashing. 'What's happening?' she asked.

But Allen didn't answer. He produced a key and unlocked the manacles. 'On your feet,' he said, and took her arm and yanked her up. 'This way.' Allen turned

Jo round and started to propel her towards the door. All at once five Primitives entered, silently coming through the door and the gaping holes that were once windows. Allen immediately pulled out his gun. 'Get out of the way,' he said menacingly.

Jo felt Allen's grip tighten on her arm, and knew that he was really nervous. 'Don't be frightened,' she said, 'they're harmless.'

Allen pushed Jo forward. 'Come on, let's go,' he said. But a Primitive stood directly in front of Allen. With his gun hand, Allen tried to shove the Primitive out of his way. Instantly, the Primitive grabbed Allen's arm, and tried to take the gun from him. Allen fired a shot, and Jo saw a Primitive by the door fall backwards, blood spurting from his chest. Everyone stopped moving; they all stood motionless, staring at the dead Primitive. Then one of the Primitives whirled round, and drove his spear into Allen's chest with a sickening thud. Allen fell backwards with a scream, the gun falling from his hand. He writhed a little then stopped moving.

Jo found herself unguarded, near the open doorway. All the Primitives were looking at Allen's body. She turned and ran. Outside the door strong arms caught her. Held fast, she looked up into the impassive face of yet another Primitive.

.   .   .   .   .

It was dawn. Winton and all the male colonists were gathered round the map. He had drawn an X to show the position of the IMC spaceship in relation to the main dome. Ashe stood forlornly in the background. The Doctor was in heated argument with Winton.

'I tell you again,' said the Doctor, 'a frontal attack would be sheer suicide!'

'We've got them outnumbered,' replied Winton.

'Do you think that means anything?' said the Doctor. 'The ship's like a fortress.'

One of the colonists, a big man called Smedley, spoke

up. 'Who's side are you really on, Doctor? If you don't want to carry a gun with us, then clear off!'

'I don't intend to carry a gun with anyone,' said the Doctor. 'All I'm suggesting is that we don't offer ourselves up to the IMC guns to get killed.'

Another colonist spoke up. 'The difference between you and us,' he told the Doctor, 'is that we saved and scrimped to get here, and we've worked with our hands to try to survive here! We're willing to die for our colony and you're not!' This outburst got a lot of approval from all the other colonists.

The Doctor waited till they'd quietened down. 'Back in the days when Earth had wars,' he said, 'there was a famous soldier called General Patton who told his men, "I don't want you to die for your country—I want you to make the enemy die for *his* country", or words to that effect. If you all get killed, as you certainly may, nothing will have been achieved.'

'All right, then,' said Winton. 'Have you got any better ideas?'

'Possibly,' said the Doctor. 'But since I suspect that there is at least one spy amongst us, I'd rather not disclose it at a public meeting.'

.   .   .   .   .

As the sun rose up gradually from the eastern horizon, Mary Ashe left the main dome and walked straight towards the IMC spaceship. She carried on one arm a small handmade basket containing a few items of food. There were now two uniformed IMC guards standing at the entrance to the spaceship. They watched her, curiously, as she walked straight towards them. As it became clear she was going to try to enter the spaceship, the guards closed in on her.

'Where do you think you're going?' one of them asked.

'I believe you've got a friend of mine here,' said Mary. 'I'm bringing her some food.'

'There are no friends of yours in this spaceship,' said the other guard, amused by his own joke.

The first guard laughed, too. Then his mouth fell open, and his body crumpled, as the Doctor, who had hidden behind the spaceship, applied a Venusian karate hold to the back of the man's neck. Winton, who had also been in hiding, simply hit the back of the other guard's head with a rock. Very quickly the two unconscious guards were dragged away.

. . . . .

Caldwell meanwhile had slept fitfully. As soon as he woke, he rolled out of his crew room bunk, pulled on his IMC uniform, and went up for'ard to the control room. Morgan and Dent were already there. 'Where's the girl?' Caldwell enquired.

Dent looked up. 'You heard me give the order last night for her to be brought here.'

Dent turned to Morgan. 'Where is she?'

'I don't know, sir,' said Morgan. 'I passed the order on to Security Guard Allen.'

Caldwell started to say, 'If you two are playing games—' but Dent cut in: 'I don't play games, Caldwell!' He turned back to Morgan. 'Find out what's happened, and be quick about it!'

Morgan reached for the console microphone, switched on and sent out a call to Security Guard Allen. After five repeated calls he turned back to Dent. 'His receiver's turned on and working, but he isn't answering.'

'Get over there,' said Dent. As Morgan scuttled out of the control room, Dent turned to Caldwell: 'If anything's happened to one of my security guards, you are to blame.'

. . . . .

Morgan went down the connecting corridor at a run. Coming from the other direction were two men in IMC

105

uniforms. 'Hey, you two,' he said, 'I want you to come with me—' And then he found himself staring into the gun drawn by the younger of the two men.

'Sorry to deceive you,' said the Doctor. 'Now turn round and go back to the control room.'

As Morgan turned, Winton thrust the gun in his back. Then Morgan heard Winton emit a quiet whistle; there was a rush of muffled footsteps as colonists swarmed through the ship's entrance and along the connecting corridors. Morgan was pushed forward to the control room. The Doctor went ahead and kicked open its door.

Winton pushed Morgan inside. Dent and Caldwell looked up, alarmed; meanwhile sounds of a gun battle between the colonists and IMC guards broke throughout the rest of the ship.

'Where's Jo Grant?' said the Doctor.

Winton was now covering the three IMC officers with the handgun he had taken from one of the overpowered guards. Dent kept his hands well in sight, for fear of being killed if Winton suspected he was reaching for his gun.

'She seems to have vanished,' said Dent, keeping very cool. This was exactly the sort of situation for which he'd been trained so well. 'I can't contact her guard. As a matter of fact, I was getting rather worried myself.'

The Doctor turned to Caldwell. 'Is he telling the truth?'

Caldwell nodded. 'I think so.'

The sound of gunfire had stopped, and the colonist Smedley came into the control room, his huge frame filling the doorway. 'Everything's under control,' he reported.

'Good,' said the Doctor. 'Winton, they're your prisoners now. I'm going to find Jo. Excuse me.' The Doctor hurried out.

Dent said, 'You realise this is an act of piracy, punishable by death under Earth's laws?'

'We're not on Earth,' replied Winton. He turned to Smedley: 'Get their guns.'

'It's a pleasure,' said Smedley, and started collecting the handguns from the three IMC officers.

.   .   .   .   .

Using a captured IMC buggy, the Doctor—now back in his own clothes—and Ashe were at the Primitive ruin in a few minutes. Security Guard Allen's body lay where it had fallen. The Doctor inspected the spear in the chest. 'It seems that the Primitives are no longer friendly,' he concluded.

Ashe was looking at the large amount of dried blood near the doorway. 'It was probably in instant retaliation,' he said. 'He shot a Primitive, and then the others turned on him.'

'Where would they have taken Jo?' asked the Doctor.

'In the early days,' said Ashe, 'two of our people said they found underground ruins in some caves. Primitives lived there, and our people got the impression that the Primitives were guarding some other sort of creature that lived down there as well. They set out again, with guns, to see what it was all about.'

'What did they find?' said the Doctor.

'We'll never know,' said Ashe. 'Neither of them ever came back.'

Ashe was about to say something else, but his voice was suddenly drowned by the thunderclap roar of a spaceship in flight. Instinctively, they both looked up. Racing across the morning sky was a spaceship similar to the IMC one but much smaller. It was coloured a brilliant scarlet.

'The Adjudicator,' said Ashe. 'That's the Earth Government colour—scarlet.'

14

The Adjudicator

Captain Dent was tied hand and foot to his captain's chair. Morgan and Caldwell were tied to their less comfortable ones. The control room was filled with colonists, and the sweaty smell of their bodies was heavy in the air that Dent had to breathe.

'You're only making things worse for yourselves,' said Dent.

Winton was busy trying to prise open a locker using a jemmy. 'You think so?'

'You heard the ship land,' Dent said. 'What sort of impression will this make on the Adjudicator?'

The colonists laughed. Winton finally broke open the locker and looked inside. 'Now what have we here?' The colonists pressed forward to see. Winton lifted out a film projector. 'What's this?' he asked Dent.

Dent thought quickly. 'Part of our survey equipment.'

But Winton found the right button to press. The projector came to life and put a picture on the wall of a giant lizard. In fact, it was a very small lizard which had been filmed in close-up. 'Just as the Doctor thought,' said Winton, 'an optical illusion.'

Smedley looked into the locker again and brought out a big metal claw. 'This is no optical illusion,' he said. 'This is what you killed the Leesons with. It's the evidence we need. You're murderers, and as of now the punishment on *our* planet is going to be death by hanging!'

All the colonists seemed to agree with this. Then Morgan spoke up. 'Captain Dent's the killer,' he said. 'He's killed colonists on other planets, too.'

Dent thought quickly. Morgan might make mistakes, but he would never act the traitor. So Dent responded, 'Shut up, Morgan!' and tried to make it sound convincing.

Winton asked Morgan, 'You want to confess?'

'I only carried out orders,' said Morgan, which was more or less true. 'I could show you more evidence if you want to see it.'

'Don't trust him,' said Smedley.

But Winton asked, 'Where is this evidence?'

'In one of the lockers here,' said Morgan. 'Untie me and I'll get it for you. You can keep a gun on me all the time.'

'You show them anything,' Dent shouted at Morgan, 'and you're finished with IMC! Understand that? You'll lose your living quarters, your wife will turn on you, your children will disown you—' One of the colonists hit Dent in the face.

Winton aimed his gun at Morgan. 'Untie him,' he told the colonists. Two of them quickly stepped forward and cut the ropes holding Morgan to his chair. He rose, and went to the most secret locker in the control room, unlocked it and put his hand inside. Now Dent had to get Winton's attention, even at the risk of another blow to the face.

'You listen to me,' Dent pleaded. 'I'm still your captain—'

Winton wheeled round, his gun pointed now at Dent. 'You're nothing!' he shouted. 'Keep quiet!'

And this gave Morgan the opportunity he needed. His hand came out of the locker holding a rocket pistol, which he pointed at the back of Winton's head. 'Drop that gun,' he said, 'or you're dead!'

To Dent it seemed a lifetime as Winton stood with his gun aimed at him, whilst Morgan stood with the rocket pistol touching Winton's head. In fact it was only three seconds before Winton realised that the colonists' victory was over, and he dropped the gun. Morgan moved Winton round, so that Winton acted as a shield against any sudden counter-attack. 'All of you,' said Morgan, 'drop your guns, or I kill this man instantly.' One by one the colonists dropped their guns to the floor. 'Now you,' he said to the colonist who had hit Dent, 'untie Captain Dent. And you,' he said to Smedley, 'untie Mr. Caldwell.'

'Drop that gun,' Morgan said, 'or you're dead!'

As soon as Dent was free he picked up a gun and levelled it at the man who had hit him. 'I should blow your head off,' he said, 'but perhaps I'll save that till later.'

Then they all heard Mary Ashe's voice from the radio loudspeaker. *'Main dome calling IMC ship,'* she said. *'The Adjudicator is ready for the tribunal. Kindly advise me the situation there.'*

Dent grabbed the microphone. '*The situation*,' he said, '*is that we are all, I repeat, all coming over there to state our case.*'

'*Who is that speaking?*' Mary asked, surprised to hear Dent. But Dent did not reply.

.　　　.　　　.　　　.　　　.

John Ashe had arranged benches along either side of the colonists' meeting-room in the dome, and one big chair at one end for the Adjudicator. The Adjudicator was already sitting there, smart in his black tunic and trousers, a small dark beard accentuating the thrust of his chin, and compelling brown eyes which darted from one to another of the colonists and IMC men as they trooped in. The colonists sat one side of the room, the IMC men sat facing them. All the colonists were unarmed; all the IMC carried holstered handguns. Captain Dent walked up to the Adjudicator, hand outstretched : 'Captain Dent, sir, at your service.'

The Adjudicator looked at Dent, but did not shake his hand. 'Please take your place,' he said.

The affront angered Dent, but he tried to cover up. 'Certainly, sir. But I thought you might first wish to see my credentials as Captain of this IMC survey team.' He produced from his pocket his plastic identity card which carried a colour photograph of himself.

The Adjudicator waved the card aside. 'I am here to settle a dispute, not to check your identity.'

'As you wish, sir,' said Dent, acutely embarrassed that these affronts had been before both the colonists and his own IMC men. 'But may I ask to see *your* identification, sir?' At last he felt that he had the Adjudicator's full attention.

'My identification?'

'Simply a formality, sir,' said Dent. 'We're on a strange planet, we've never met before . . . it seems a reasonable request.'

'I am the Adjudicator,' said the Adjudicator severely, 'for this section of the galaxy. Now kindly be seated.'

Dent turned and sat next to Morgan. He touched the younger man's arm :

'Good work, Morgan. I'll see IMC know how you acted today.' Morgan smiled, but nudged Dent to pay attention to the Adjudicator. Dent turned to see the Adjudicator rising to his feet.

'I understand you two groups of people are in dispute,' said the Adjudicator. 'By the powers vested in me by the Earth Government, I shall endeavour to reach a just decision. I shall first hear from the plaintiffs, who are the colonists.' Suddenly he smiled. 'May I suggest that for all our sakes, brevity should be the key-note? Now then, Mr. John Ashe.'

Ashe was not brief. He described every detail of the events which had led up to this tribunal. Dent was pleased to see that the Adjudicator was clearly bored with Ashe's digressions and general wordiness. Finally, much to everyone's relief, Ashe sat down.

The Adjudicator said, 'Is there any proof of these terrible accusations?'

Winton jumped up : 'We found it in their spaceship—the metal claw they used to kill the Leesons, and a projector—'

The Adjudicator cut in : 'Can you produce this evidence now?'

'They've destroyed it,' said Winton.

The Adjudicator pulled on his little beard. 'Then it's very difficult for me to believe that these things ever existed.' Before the colonists could protest, however, the Adjudicator turned to Dent. 'I will now hear the case for IMC, Captain Dent.'

Dent stood up. 'Believing this planet to be assigned for mining,' he said, trying to be as brief as possible in order to please the Adjudicator, 'we landed on it. When we found unlawful colonists, we sought your help. Meanwhile, the colonists attacked us, and for a short time held us prisoner in our own ship. Thus they have put themselves outside the law. I submit that these people be ordered to leave this planet immediately.' He sat down.

The Adjudicator beamed with pleasure. Clearly Dent's presentation of his case had gone down well. 'Is that *all* you have to say, Captain Dent?'

'Yes, sir,' said Dent. 'Except that this planet is rich in minerals which could make homes for millions of people on Earth.'

Ashe jumped up. 'That is an irrelevant argument! The only question at issue is our legal position, not who needs what minerals!'

'Really?' said the Adjudicator. 'Do the needs of people on Earth mean nothing to you, Mr. Ashe?'

Ashe was flustered. 'Yes, I mean, no—well, what I mean is, sir, it's not what we're discussing.'

'Thank you,' said the Adjudicator, 'I do like to be told what I am allowed to discuss! Now kindly sit down, Mr. Ashe.'

Ashe sat down, his face red with embarrassment.

'I have heard the statements from both sides,' said the Adjudicator. 'On my way here I contacted Earth and had a check made on planetary records. Undoubtedly, an error has occurred. A faulty computer on Earth has assigned this planet both for colonists *and* for mining. So it is left entirely to me to decide. However, this is a weighty decision, one that I shall need to consider. This tribunal stands temporarily adjourned.' He stood up. 'It is customary to remain seated until I depart. I shall return now to my spaceship, and shall re-convene this tribunal in due course.'

But Ashe was on his feet. 'Sir, I implore you! The lives of all my friends depend on your decision! Can't you tell us right away?'

'Kindly be seated,' snapped the Adjudicator. Then he strode out of the dome.

Everybody got up now, and in the general jumble of colonists and IMC men, Dent found himself facing Ashe. Ashe looked bewildered, on the verge of tears. As though forgetting that Dent was his enemy, Ashe said, 'I think that Adjudicator's got some strange streak of cruelty in him, to keep us on tenterhooks like this.'

Dent did not reply because he never spoke to colonists unless it was necessary. But he agreed with what Ashe had said. There was something very strange about this Adjudicator.

15

Primitive City

It was not difficult for the Doctor to follow the tracks made by the six-toed Primitives and their prisoner, Jo. The tracks led fairly directly from the ruin where he had left John Ashe, and the outcrop of rocky hills on the other side of the section of flat desert. The foot tracks eventually converged with the drag marks of the TARDIS : the combination of the two brought the Doctor to what appeared to be a solid rock face. He concluded that there must be some kind of door in this rock face, and started to look for it.

From the distance he heard the pounding of running feet. He turned to see a group of Primitives racing towards him across the desert, spears raised. There was nowhere to hide, and these strange half-men could outrun even the Doctor. He waited, with his back to the cliff face. Then the Primitives were all around him.

'I have come here to take back the girl,' he said. 'You may not understand my words, but I know you can read my mind. I am willing to buy the girl back with exciting and interesting bits of machinery. There is also a tall blue box which happens to belong to me . . .' But he was interrupted by one of the Primitives suddenly going up to the rock face and nodding his head towards it. To the Doctor's astonishment, a concealed door in the rock opened. 'How very kind of you,' said the Doctor as he was thrust inside, then partly dragged, partly pushed, down a long corridor with rock walls. Some distance along the corridor there was an opening in one of the walls. As the Doctor went by he glanced through the opening and for a moment caught a glimpse of a vista of strange machinery, silent and unattended. The Doctor wanted to stop, but the Primitives pushed him forward. Presently the corridor ended with a T-junction. The Primitives turned to the right, dragging and pushing the Doctor with them. From this point on, the Doctor found himself being taken through a maze of turns and forks, and he desperately tried to commit the route to memory. Finally, they arrived at a door set in the rock, a door with a heavy metal bolt. One of the Primitives pulled aside the bolt, and the Doctor was thrust into a room cut in the rock. Jo was standing there.

'Doctor!' She rushed forward and flung her arms around him.

'Now just a minute, Jo,' he said, 'I want to try to talk, or at least think, to these fellows.' The Doctor turned but the door had already been slammed shut. 'I can't say much for their hospitality,' he muttered.

'They've probably gone to get the other one,' Jo said.

'What other one?' asked the Doctor.

'There's a sort of creature,' she said, 'that seems to be in charge of them.'

'Humanoid?' asked the Doctor.

'No,' she said, 'not really. At least, it's got a horrible face, like an animal.'

'It might have a horrible face to you,' said the Doctor, 'but to itself it might be rather good-looking.'

'You haven't seen it,' she said. 'Anyway, how do we get out of here?'

'No worry about that,' said the Doctor. 'I'm here to buy you back. Just a simple business transaction. Ashe says it's happened before.' He started to look round the room. At one end there was a machine, rather like a clock with all its parts showing. The Doctor examined it, and realised that, whatever its purpose, it hadn't actually worked for centuries. 'This room, and this machinery,' he said, 'must have been part of a highly-advanced civilisation, once.'

Jo said, 'Then what's happened to it?'

'Somehow it must have gone into decline,' conjectured

the Doctor. 'Those people we call the Primitives may be the descendants of a tremendously advanced race.'

'I've been looking at this over here,' Jo said, leading the Doctor to the other side of the room. 'Look.'

Jo pointed to a series of pictures that ran along all of one wall, and the Doctor inspected them with mounting interest. The pictures were very old and badly faded, but it was possible to see that each depicted something about the life of human-type people in a well-ordered community. 'Look at this first one,' said the Doctor with excitement, 'men dragging a heavy piece of stone. Yet here,' he said, pointing to the next picture, 'are men dragging a wheeled vehicle with a heavy weight on it.'

'They'd invented the wheel,' said Jo.

'And here,' said the Doctor, moving along the series of pictures, 'is more complicated machinery—the water-pump, the steam engine, and now machines that can fly in the air.'

'That's progress,' said Jo. 'Do you notice one thing?— three different types of people.'

'Yes, I'd noticed that,' said the Doctor. 'The three seem to start here,' he said, pointing to a picture that seemed to indicate the discovery of electronic science. 'In the beginning all men were equal, but now we have lots of people drawn like match-stick men, and they're probable workers lightly dressed or with no clothes at all; then these figures in robes . . .'

'The creature with the horrible face had a long robe,' Jo cut in.

'They may be some kind of priest,' said the Doctor. 'And now one or two very tiny figures.'

'Like babies,' said Jo.

'Or dolls,' said the Doctor. 'Ashe told me how a Primitive became very excited when Mary Ashe happened to produce a doll.'

'What's happening here?' said Jo, pointing to a picture a long way along the series. It showed buildings in ruins, and the match-stick figures lying on top of one another in a heap.

'Some terrible catastrophe,' said the Doctor. 'Notice how the artist's style is cruder here, more primitive. Look at this one.' It was the last picture in the frieze. Priest-like figures were pushing a doll figure through a door, beyond which were flames.'

'A sacrifice,' said Jo.

The Doctor nodded. 'To some machine which had a furnace.' He heard the bolt in the door outside being drawn back, and turned round. The door opened slowly. A creature with a human body and a hairy otter-like face entered. It was dressed in long robes. Immediately behind it came six Primitives, all with spears. Jo moved over to the Doctor and clung to his arm. 'How do you do?' said the Doctor. 'I'm here to take back this young lady. In return I shall give you interesting bits of machinery . . .'

The otter-like face peered round the room, blindly. Then it gestured to the Primitives. Four of the Primitives dropped their spears and came forward to grab the Doctor and Jo.

'I come here in peace,' said the Doctor. 'I mean you no harm!'

Already his arms were pinioned behind his back by a hugely powerful Primitive. The robed creature gestured again, and Jo and the Doctor were hustled out of the room and down what seemed endless corridors cut in the rock. They arrived at enormous double-doors guarded by more Primitives. These were opened and Jo and the Doctor were pushed into a large room. This was different from any other part of the underground city. Instead of rough-rock walls, the sides were made of smooth, silvery-coloured metal. In the centre was a large round object like a drum made of the same silvery metal. On its top were press-button controls.

'It's very kind of you to show us all this,' said the Doctor, as though he had entered the room voluntarily. 'What's that?' Since his arms were still firmly held behind his back, he could only indicate the drum object by nodding his head. Neither the Primitives nor the robed creature took any notice of the Doctor's remarks. They pushed him to the far end of the room where a large hatch was let into the wall. The robed creature looked at the hatch with its near-sightless eyes, then gestured again. The Primitive who had been on guard outside sprang forward and opened the hatch. Intense heat filled the room. Inside the hatch was a white-hot electronic furnace.

'They're going to sacrifice us!' Jo screamed.

As the Doctor struggled wildly to free himself, four Primitives dragged Jo towards the hatch. Her screams filled the room, echoing from the metal walls, as they picked her up bodily to throw her into the furnace. Then, suddenly, a small doll-like creature seemed to swim up from the flames, its tiny white hand raised. The Primitives dropped Jo and backed away in terror. The robed creature looked about blindly, not knowing what had happened. The Doctor found his arms released, and the Primitives who had held him began backing away from the creature that had materialised from the furnace.

'I am the Guardian,' said the little doll figure that seemed to float in the flames. 'Why have you entered this place?'

'I was brought here,' answered Jo.

'And I came to take her back,' said the Doctor. 'May I ask what it is that you guard?'

The Guardian ignored the Doctor's question. 'All intruders in this city must die. That is the law.'

'The race who built this city,' said the Doctor urgently, 'were intelligent and civilised. Their laws would not condemn the innocent.'

'The law must be obeyed,' said the Guardian.

'Surely all true laws must be based on justice?' the Doctor argued. 'We are strangers to this planet. All we ask is to be allowed to go.'

The Guardian seemed to consider this point. Then it spoke again: 'You are of superior intelligence, so you may go free.'

'*I am the Guardian,*' said the little doll figure that seemed to float in the flames.

Jo hugged the Doctor. 'Thanks,' she said to the Guardian.

'But you,' the Guardian said to Jo, 'are of no value. I shall give you to the servants for a sacrifice. It amuses them.'

'I refuse to leave without her,' said the Doctor. 'I am responsible for her safety.'

'And I,' said the Guardian, 'am responsible for the safety of that which I guard.'

'Does the amusement of your servants warrant the death of an intelligent being?' said the Doctor.

Again the Guardian seemed to weigh up the Doctor's words before answering. 'I was sacrificed, and I still live.'

'Not all are like you,' said the Doctor, 'so that is no argument.'

'I appreciate logic,' said the Guardian. 'Is this creature you protect of some value?'

'She is life,' said the Doctor. 'That which is living is always of value. It cannot be replaced.'

'Therefore,' said the Guardian, who seemed to be enjoying this debate, 'do you not eat?'

'I regret, sir,' said the Doctor, 'I do not understand your question.'

'If you eat flesh then the life of that flesh ceases to exist,' said the Guardian.

Jo clung to the Doctor's arm. 'Tell him we'll be vegetarians from now on.'

'I understand your remark,' said the Guardian. 'But if one eats vegetation, that too dies. What is your answer to that?'

Jo whispered desperately to the Doctor. 'Doctor, just plead for my life! I have a right to live!'

'It's no good,' whispered the Doctor. 'The Guardian only understands logic. Leave this to me.' He turned back to the little doll creature that floated in the white hot flames. 'I concede your point, Guardian. All nature kills to eat, but that is for the purpose of continuing life in another form. To throw this girl into those flames would be to extinguish life totally.'

The Guardian thought for a full minute before replying. 'You make good argument. Both of you may now leave. You will not be harmed.' Slowly the Guardian faded back into the flames.

Within an hour the Doctor and Jo had safely emerged from the Primitive City and driven across the flat desert back to the colonists' dome. The Doctor first knew things had changed when an armed IMC guard stepped forward from the entrance to the dome and said, 'That buggy is IMC property.' The Doctor gladly dismounted from the vehicle. 'I had every intention to return it,' he said.

'The tribunal's re-convened,' said the guard. 'Why not go in and hear what the Adjudicator's decided?' He pointed his gun menacingly at the Doctor.

'I take it,' said the Doctor, 'that you've all got your guns back?'

'You take it right,' said the guard, and pushed the Doctor with the nozzle of his gun.

The Doctor said, 'This way, Jo,' and led her by the hand into the main meeting room. All the colonists sat on one side, the IMC men on the other. As the Doctor entered he stopped and stared at the man seated on the large chair at the end of the room. All eyes were on the man as he spoke:

'During the adjournment I have considered the evidence very carefully. While I have sympathy with the colonists, there is no proof at all that their colony is successful. Crops refuse to grow, and animal life is hostile...'

Winton jumped up. 'That was all faked by the IMC men!'

The man in the big chair ignored the interruption and continued: 'What's more, the colonists have behaved badly by attacking the IMC spaceship. They have made allegations which they cannot prove. In view of this, and the fact that this planet has a mineral needed by Earth, I rule that this planet is unsuitable for colonisation. The colonists must leave at the earliest possible time. Kindly all remain seated while I exit.'

In the stunned silence which followed, the man rose from the big chair and walked towards where the Doctor and Jo were standing by the entrance. He beamed at the Doctor, but knew better than to offer his hand.

'How interesting to see you here, Doctor,' he said.

'And what,' asked the Doctor, 'are you, the Master, doing on *this* planet?'

The Master dropped his voice. ' "Adjudicator", if you don't mind,' he said. 'Now, if you'll excuse me, it is my duty as the Adjudicator to have a private word with the losing side and explain how they can appeal.'

'Your *duty?*' said the Doctor, hardly believing his ears.

'Of course,' said the Master. 'A question of justice and

fairness.' He turned to John Ashe. 'Mr. Ashe, are you ready for a private talk with me?'

The Master turned on his heel and went off towards Ashe's private quarters. Ashe rose from the bench he shared with the other colonists and slowly followed. Then the IMC men rose and trooped out of the dome. Winton jumped to his feet. 'That Adjudicator was bribed by IMC,' he said loudly. The colonists gathered round him to listen. 'We've given up our homes and secure jobs on Earth to find a better life on this planet. Are you going to let some crooked Adjudicator rob you of all that?'

'I understand,' said the Doctor, 'that there is the possibility of an appeal. Won't you let your leader try to use legal methods?'

'The law is the law of Earth Government,' shouted Winton. 'I vote we break with Earth altogether, and declare ourselves an independent democratic republic!'

There was a murmur of strong approval from the crowd of colonists. The big man, Smedley, stepped into the middle of the circle next to Winton. 'He's right. Those of you willing to carry arms against IMC and Earth, follow me and be counted!' He walked to the end of the room, and immediately Winton followed. 'Well,' called Winton, 'who's for freedom?'

The colonists looked at one another uncertainly. What Winton and Smedley proposed was treason against Earth Government. Then one man left the main body of the colonists and went to join Winton and Smedley. 'You're right,' the man said, 'we've had enough. I'll fight.'

Jo appealed to the Doctor. 'You must stop them, Doctor. They'll be outlaws.'

'I know,' said the Doctor. 'But how can I say anything when I really agree with them?'

Now two more men stepped forward to join those standing at the far end of the room. 'What about some of you women?' Winton called; and first two, then three, then five women joined Winton and Smedley and the others. 'And you men,' shouted Smedley, 'are you

123

still undecided?' All the remaining men moved up to the end of the room, followed by all the women except Mary Ashe. She now stood alone where the group had been.

'Mary,' said Winton, 'which side are you on? IMC's or ours?'

'My father will try to get us justice,' she said.

'The only justice we'll get,' said Smedley, 'is with guns!'

Mary suddenly burst into tears and ran down one of the corridors so that the others would not see her cry. The colonists formed a close circle round Winton and Smedley and started to discuss their next move against IMC.

'There'll be more killing,' said Jo.

'Of course,' said the Doctor, 'but the situation is out of our hands now. Our real problem is the Master. He's come to this planet for some reason, and I've got to find out what it is.'

16

The Ambush

Captain Dent opened the locker in his control room that contained the officers' supply of astrobeer and synthetic champagne. He was happy to be back in the IMC ship, where he felt secure from the wide open spaces of this miserable planet. 'Tell the crew it's stand-easy,' he said to Morgan, 'and they can all have an issue of champagne, too.' He opened a can of champagne and offered it to Caldwell.

'Some other time,' said Caldwell.

'Take it,' said Dent. To him the can of champagne was a peace offering, to show Caldwell he was willing to forget their past disagreements. 'We're friends, aren't we?'

This, as Dent knew it would, appealed to Caldwell's basic good nature. He took the can, but he didn't drink straight away. 'Thanks.'

Dent got out cans for himself and Morgan. 'Maybe we did have to play it rough,' he said to Caldwell. 'But the trouble's over now. Those colonists will find another planet, perhaps better than this one.'

The radio loudspeaker crackled. *'This is the Adjudicator,'* said an almost inaudible voice. *'I have received an emergency call and must leave this planet immediately. I wish to meet Captain Dent and his officers in the colonists' dome straight away. The settlement must be ratified in the presence of all parties.'* The transmission ended.

Dent looked at Morgan and Caldwell. 'Hold the champagne till later,' he said. 'Let's go.' He pulled on his gunbelt and led the way.

A hundred yards away, in the colonists' dome, Smedley asked Winton, 'Do you think you fooled them?' Winton put down the radio-microphone. 'We'll soon know.' He looked at the armed colonists surrounding him. 'Get in your positions. And shoot to kill!'

Down a corridor within the dome, the Doctor and Jo were listening, ears pressed to the thin partition wall, to a conversation between Ashe and the Master.

'Believe me, my dear Ashe,' said the Master, 'I sympathise with your position. But I have no choice. However, you have a right to appeal.'

'On what grounds?' said Ashe.

For a moment the Doctor and Jo heard nothing. Then it was the Master's voice again, after a long and effective pause. 'If this planet had some historical interest, for instance.'

Ashe said, 'There was once a great civilisation here, so I believe.'

'Indeed?' said the Master. 'Any traces left?'

'There's a ruined underground city not far from here,' said Ashe.

There was a sudden urgency in the Master's voice. 'Could you lead me to it?'

'It's dangerous,' said Ashe. 'The Primitives don't like people going there.'

'Do you know why?' asked the Master.

'I think there's something of great importance to them there,' said Ashe.

'I imagine there is,' said the Master. 'Indeed, the sooner I get there the better.'

Elsewhere in the dome, concealed behind a packing-case, Norton pulled his tiny two-way radio from his pocket and desperately tried to contact the IMC ship to warn them. But the message was never sent. Smedley, who was deploying men for the ambush, came upon Norton with the two-way radio in his hand. 'Norton,' said Smedley, not yet having seen the radio, 'I want you and two other fellows to hide . . .' Then he saw the radio. 'That's an IMC transmitter,' he shouted. Norton knew this could never be explained away. He tried to dive between Smedley's legs to escape. Smedley's great hands came down on Norton's neck and broke it. Norton's body fell limp to the ground. Smedley stamped on the little two-way radio until all its parts were spewed out on the floor; then he went on with his work of organising the ambush.

Five minutes later the IMC officers, followed by their guards, strode into the dome. No one was to be seen. 'Adjudicator!' called Captain Dent, 'you wanted us back here to ratify the settlement.' By now all the IMC guards had crowded in behind Dent and Morgan, forming a neat target for the guns of the hidden colonists. At a shout from Winton, armed colonists appeared from behind the agricultural machinery, the packing-cases, the door leading to the radio room, from over the railings of the steps that led to upstairs quarters. Three IMC guards died instantly in the initial hail of bullets; the others, with Dent and Morgan, dived for protective positions and returned the fire.

The Doctor and Jo rushed along the corridor from Ashe's private quarters to the scene of the battle, the Doctor hoping he might be able to call for a cease-fire to stop the bloodshed. The Master, who had also heard the shooting, hurriedly left John Ashe: it would upset all his plans if the colonists' revolt was successful.

Keeping Jo well back, the Doctor stood in a doorway that led on to the scene of the battle. 'For the sake of reason,' he called, 'stop shooting!' And then he felt a gun rammed into the back of his own neck.

'Sorry, Doctor,' said the Master, 'but an opportunity such as this cannot be missed.' He moved round the Doctor, still holding his small handgun aimed at the Doctor's head. 'I'd rather be watching your face as I pull the trigger,' he said.

'You'd kill me in cold blood?'

'On the contrary,' replied the Master, 'you are going to die in the heat of battle. A stray bullet, from an IMC or a colonist's gun—no one will ever really know. Goodbye, Doctor.'

The Master raised the gun and started to squeeze the trigger. John Ashe came running down the corridor. 'Adjudicator,' he shouted, 'we've got to stop this! My people are making themselves into outlaws!'

'Exactly what I was saying to the Doctor,' said the Master, lowering the gun. He could hardly murder the Doctor in front of Ashe. 'Perhaps you'd like to tell them to stop.'

Both the Master and the Doctor took cover as an IMC man ran to the doorway for cover, and was cut down by a volley of fire from partly hidden colonists. The IMC man fell against John Ashe, knocking him backwards. Ashe struggled to get up again, but the IMC man lay where he was, dead.

'Stop shooting!' It was Captain Dent's voice, shouting from behind a crate of seed. His hand came into sight waving a white handkerchief. 'We give in.' Almost at once the shooting stopped.

'Stand up,' shouted Winton from his hiding-place. 'Tell your men to drop their guns.'

For a few seconds nothing happened—no shots, and the men on both sides still lying concealed. Then Captain Dent slowly stood up and threw his gun on to the ground. He was white with the fear that some colonist might take this golden opportunity to shoot him.

'We are heavily outnumbered,' Dent called. 'I order all IMC personnel to lay down their guns immediately.'

Now Winton stood up, too. 'You must radio your men in your spaceship,' he called to Dent, 'and tell them of your surrender. If they refuse, you and all your men here will be killed.' He turned to the colonists. 'Round up the prisoners, and collect their guns.'

Everyone came out of hiding now, the IMC men with their hands raised. The women emerged and started to tend the wounded. Winton caught sight of the Master with Ashe and the Doctor and came over to them, his gun on the Master. 'We've had enough of you, too,' he said to the Master. 'You'll leave with the IMC men.'

The Master, quickly slipping his own gun out of sight,

smiled at Winton. 'I don't think you understand the position you are now in,' he said. 'Unless you want Earth Government to send a space fleet to blow you out of the skies, you need someone to negotiate for you.'

Ashe said, 'You'd still be willing to help us, Adjudicator?'

'Of course,' said the Master. 'You've acted rashly, but I am impressed by your courage and determination.'

'Don't listen to him,' said the Doctor. 'He's trying to trick you.'

But the Master continued, ignoring the Doctor. 'There may be a case for preserving your colony on the grounds of the planet's historical interest. If I could investigate this claim, things might be very different. I should like to visit the Primitive City.'

'I am trying to warn you,' said the Doctor to Ashe and Winton, 'this man is not to be trusted. He is an impostor. You should check his credentials with Earth!'

They stepped back as a group of prisoners, which included Morgan, were led away by Smedley and other colonists.

'May I ask, sir,' said the Master to the Doctor, 'exactly who you are?'

Both Winton and Ashe looked at the Doctor. 'Yes,' said Winton, 'you've never really explained yourself.'

The Master put his arms round Ashe's and Winton's shoulders. 'Gentlemen, I suggest that we continue our discussion uninterrupted. Now let us go somewhere private to consider how I might intercede on your behalf with Earth Government.' And with that the Master led Ashe and Winton away from the Doctor.

'Doctor,' said Jo, 'you've got to stop him. He's going to talk them into believing him!'

'There may be another way,' said the Doctor. 'Come on.' He strode out of the dome. Jo, not understanding, quickly followed him.

17

Captain Dent Thinks Twice

'Maintain parking orbit!'

Captain Dent barked the order to the IMC technicians in the control room. They made the necessary adjustments and the IMC ship levelled off in its ascent from the planet and went into a wide orbit.

Morgan entered. 'I've checked the stores,' he told Dent. 'They've taken our buggies, all our guns and ammunition, even our rocket pistols. They also took all our mining explosives.'

Caldwell looked across from where he had watched Dent pilot the ship back up into Space. 'How's the astrobeer supply and the stocks of victory champagne?' he asked, not expecting an answer. The others ignored him.

Morgan said, 'What do we do now, Captain Dent?'

'Stay in parking orbit,' said Dent, 'and radio IMC on Earth for a gunship.'

'Is that going to look good on our work records,' said Morgan, 'asking for help?'

Dent turned to him. 'Have you got any other ideas?' It wasn't a question, more of an expression of despair.

'As a matter of fact,' said Morgan, 'there was one strange thing. When I was being led out as a prisoner, that man the Doctor called the Adjudicator an impostor.'

Dent gave thought to that. 'You remember,' he said at last, 'when I first met the Adjudicator he refused to show me his identity card. I wonder . . .' Suddenly he grabbed the radio-microphone and within a few moments was talking to the Identification Tracing Department of IMC on Earth. He explained nothing of what had happened, he simply asked for an identity check on the Adjudicator of this section of the galaxy, a routine enquiry which could not reflect badly on Captain Dent in any way. Ten minutes later, in reply to Dent's query, a telephoto picture started to be printed line by line on the ship's telephoto machine. Dent and Morgan watched with increasing interest as the face appeared. It was round, chubby, the eyes were blue, the hair fair, and there was no beard. Caldwell looked at the picture over Dent's shoulder.

'Well, well,' said Caldwell, 'I guess we all got fooled.'

'Had we better report this to Earth?' said Morgan.

'No,' said Dent. He had no intention of letting IMC on Earth know that he'd been tricked. 'We'll handle this ourselves.'

'Without guns?' Morgan asked, and Dent noticed how Morgan had stopped calling him 'sir' since things had gone against them.

'We shall have to be a bit craftier,' said Dent. He turned to the technicians. 'Prepare to go into landing orbit!'

As the IMC ship gently sank back onto the planet, cushioned by its retro-rockets, Captain Dent saw the sun tipping the western horizon. They landed in a small valley 35 kilometres from the colonists' dome. Finally, the ship steadied as it touched down on the planet's surface, and the motors were shut off.

'And now we wait,' said Captain Dent. 'Even without buggies, we can reach the colonists within four hours. We shall wait until night.'

18

The Master's TARDIS

The Doctor and Jo stood outside the scarlet ship in which the Master had arrived on the planet. 'It's just an ordinary spaceship,' remarked Jo, 'like the IMC one, only smaller.'

The Doctor produced a key from his pocket. 'We shall soon know,' he said, and tried the key in what seemed to be the only entrance hatch in the ship's side. The key turned easily.

'How did you get that key?' Jo asked.

The Doctor winked. 'Oh, from a previous encounter I had with the Master. Anyway, it works.' He pulled open the hatch and they went inside.

Jo looked about in astonishment. Except for minor differences, it was exactly like the inside of the Doctor's TARDIS. 'It *is* a TARDIS,' she said. 'Why did you want to come here?'

'To see what I can find,' said the Doctor evasively. 'Now be careful!' He put a hand on Jo's shoulder to stop her going forward, and with the other hand pointed to a small white light in the wall close to them. The light shone a beam on to an electroplate opposite. 'A rather crude burglar alarm,' said the Doctor, 'let's duck under it.'

They crawled on hands and knees under the beam of light, then stood up. 'What do you hope to find?' said Jo.

The Doctor was already looking in cupboards and drawers. 'Something that might tell me why the Master has come to this planet,' he said. 'You try that filing-cabinet,' he said, pointing to a set of deep drawers.

Jo looked through the files. 'Do you think he's after that duralinium stuff, like the IMC people?' she asked. But the Doctor was too busy making his own search, or didn't think the question worth answering. Jo shrugged, and continued searching through the files. Then she came across a folder containing a plastic document bearing a colour photograph of a clean-shaven man with a round chubby face, blue eyes, and fair hair. Wording on the document stated that it had been issued by the Bureau of Interplanetary Affairs and described the bearer, one Martin Jurgens, as an official Adjudicator. 'I think this is worth looking at,' Jo said, showing the document to the Doctor. 'It's the man the Master is impersonating.'

The Doctor looked sadly at the photograph. 'Poor Martin Jurgens, whoever he was, is probably floating for all eternity in Space, or atomised.'

'Well, come on,' said Jo, 'let's take that and show it to Mr. Ashe.' In her eagerness as she made for the door her legs passed through the beam of light . . .

*   *   *   *   *

At that moment a bleep-bleep sound came from a pocket in the Master's tunic. He was with John Ashe in the latter's quarters in the dome, and together they were studying some crude maps which Ashe had drawn of the area of the colony.

'Excuse me,' said the Master with a smile, and drew from his pocket a small black box that fitted neatly into his palm. He opened a panel in the box, revealing a tiny television screen. On it he could clearly see the Doctor and Jo in his TARDIS. He didn't let Ashe see the screen.

'What's that?' said Ashe.

'A useful little device,' said the Master. 'A remote-control alarm in case someone tampers with my space-ship. Probably one of the Primitives touched the outside of the craft. It's of no importance.' He closed the panel. 'Now then, Mr. Ashe, you were telling me about the underground Primitive City? . . .'

As the Master returned the little black box into his pocket, his thumb gently squeezed a button in its side.

. * * ? . .

'Come on, Doctor,' said Jo, 'what I found is enough to prove to Mr. Ashe that the Master isn't the Adjudicator. Let's go before the Master comes and catches us here.'

The Doctor straightened up from the drawers he had been searching. 'All right, Jo.' He turned, then froze. 'Jo! You've crossed back through the alarm beam!'

And already the button on the side of the Master's little alarm box had activated poisonous gas to be pumped into the TARDIS. It came through six grills set near the floor, and it came under pressure. Its effect was to be almost instantaneous. The ship's only exit door automatically closed.

Half-an-hour later the Doctor started to come to. He was lying where he had fallen, looking up into the Master's face. The Master had an aerosol spray in his hand, aimed at the Doctor. 'A little device to speed up the recovery of those overcome by my sleeping gas,' said the Master, now putting aside the aerosol spray can. 'How are you feeling?'

The Doctor had a sick headache. He looked round for Jo. 'Where is Miss Grant?' he asked.

'Over there,' said the Master. He pointed to a tall upright glass cubicle. Jo was inside, sitting on the floor with her head between her legs. 'She's perfectly safe,' said the Master, '*and* secure. In a short time she'll sleep off that whiff of gas and wake up. However,' he continued, producing his bleep-bleep box, 'this little gadget has more than one control. The black button is for sleeping gas. But the red button, once pressed, would fill Miss Grant's glass case with nerve gas. She would die within a few minutes of total paralysis.' He put the little black box into his tunic pocket. 'Now Doctor, I understand you've visited the Primitives' underground city. I want you to take me there.'

The Doctor slowly got to his feet. '*That's* the real reason for your coming to this planet, isn't it?'

'Possibly,' said the Master. 'Shall we go?'

The Doctor was lying where he had fallen, looking up into the Master's face.

'The Primitives don't like intruders,' said the Doctor. 'It may be dangerous.'

'You've been there and come out alive,' said the Master. 'In any case, concern yourself solely with Miss Grant's welfare. *And* mine. So remember, if any harm comes to me, I shall press that red button.' He went to the door and held it open for the Doctor. 'One thing puzzles me, though. How did you get into my TARDIS?'

'Without difficulty,' said the Doctor, avoiding a

direct answer, and hoping that the Master wasn't going to press the point.

'Well,' said the Master, 'you were still caught by the burglar alarm, so not to worry.' They were outside now and he stopped to close and lock the hatch. With the Master's back turned, the Doctor quietly dropped the key on the soft dusty soil at his feet, in the hope that someone might find it. The Master turned back to him, pocketing his own key. 'All right then, Doctor, lead me to the Primitives' underground city!'

'What is it you want there?' asked the Doctor, genuinely puzzled.

'What have I ever wanted?' replied the Master. 'Power! Complete and total power! And through you, Doctor, I am going to get it.'

19

The Return of Captain Dent

John Ashe lay in bed, trying to read in order to calm his troubled mind. He had brought two books with him from Earth : one was on agriculture, from the days before all Earth's food was taken from the seas; the other was a copy of something written thousands of years ago, and was largely about someone called God. It was this second book he now tried to read, not because he really understood it, but because the strange language fascinated him. It contained four versions of a story about a man who sacrificed his own life for the the sake of others. It was this part of the book that most interested Ashe, because it was so difficult to understand. Why, he asked himself, should anyone willingly give his own life for other people? His thinking was interrupted by Winton and Smedley entering his sleeping quarters.

'Where's the Adjudicator?' said Winton.

Ashe put down the book. 'Why do you want him?'

'We're sending him back to Earth,' said Smedley, 'right now.'

'But he may be able to help us,' Ashe said. 'Although he took a decision against us, he is really a fair man. He believes we may have grounds for an appeal.'

'He's twisted you round his little finger,' Winton said. 'Where's he gone?'

Ashe knew it was no good arguing. 'To his spaceship. He said he was going to meet the Doctor there.'

'That's another one we want off this planet,' said Smedley. 'We've never really known where he came from.'

Ashe hoped they would leave him now, but they had

other pressing business. 'We want those IMC guns,' said Winton. They lay in a crate next to Ashe's bed.

'You've no need for them,' said Ashe. 'You've already got your own guns.'

'Ours are like pea-shooters compared with the IMC guns,' said Winton. 'What if Earth Government sends soldiers?—we'll need high-powered guns then.'

'If that happens,' Ashe said, 'I'll issue them. But if the Adjudicator helps us it will never come to that.'

'Yes,' said Smedley, '*if*.'

'You know I'm the leader now,' said Winton. 'Those guns should be under my authority!'

'Except,' said Ashe, 'I happen to have them in here. So get out of my quarters!'

Winton and Smedley turned and went away, slamming the door of Ashe's sleeping room. Ashe got up from his bed to lock the door, to make sure Winton couldn't come back when Ashe was asleep to take the guns. Then he had second thoughts. Doors were never locked in the dome, except to stop the Primitives from stealing their scarce food supplies. If Winton found the door locked, it would be thought an aggressive act by Ashe. And Ashe believed that with patience he could win back the support of the colonists. He knew Winton meant well, but the colony needed Ashe's calmness and maturity. He got back onto his bed, and tried once more to read his book.

There was a gentle tap on the door. 'Come in,' he called, hoping it was Winton so that they could make friends again. There was another tap. 'I said "come in",' he called. Suddenly the door burst open and Morgan and Captain Dent rushed into the room and pinioned Ashe on his bed before he could move. The room seemed suddenly full with the black uniforms of IMC guards as they helped themselves to their high-powered weapons. A moment later, Ashe heard shots from the colonists' shotguns down the corridor. An IMC guard reeled into the room, shot in the head. Other IMC guards took up defensive positions in the doorway and returned the fire.

Dent held a handgun at Ashe's head and Morgan went to the door and called to the colonists: 'Stop firing or we kill Ashe!'

The firing continued, and Ashe wondered if none of the colonists now cared whether he lived or died. Morgan called again, this time louder: 'Stop firing or we kill Ashe on the count of three. One, two . . .' The firing abruptly stopped.

Still holding the gun at Ashe's head, Dent ordered: 'Have all the colonists in the outlying domes brought in for the trial.'

Morgan went away to carry out Dent's orders.

'Trial?' said Ashe. 'What trial?'

'The Adjudicator's decision made me legal Governor of this planet,' said Dent. 'You will be charged with armed rebellion against Earth Government. Under the law, every man who carried a gun can be executed.'

'You'd never do that,' said Ashe. 'The ordinary people on Earth would be horrified. They'd turn against IMC, and make the Earth Government disown you!'

Dent smiled. 'Perhaps you've got a point there,' he said, putting away his gun now all danger was over. 'So I might give you an alternative.' The smile suddenly faded: 'You can pack yourself and all your colonist friends into that old spaceship of yours and get off this planet!'

'Our spaceship can never make another journey,' said Ashe, 'it's too old. Don't you realise what may happen?'

'Every year,' said Dent, 'thousands of people are killed in accidents. My only concern is the good name of IMC. Whatever happens to you all once you're off this planet, it can't reflect on us.'

Morgan returned. 'Captain Dent, sir,' he said—Dent noted with satisfaction that Morgan had started calling him 'sir' again—'the guards are rounding up all the colonists. I've also searched the dome for that fake Adjudicator but he isn't here.'

Ashe said, 'Did you say *fake* Adjudicator?'

Dent was amused. 'Of course, you're hoping that he'll

help you people against us! Sorry, but you'll get no assistance from that direction. I want to find out who he is and what his game is. Where is he?'

'I don't know,' Ashe lied. He had no reason to believe anything Dent said.

'Or don't you want to tell us,' said Dent. He turned back to Morgan: 'Go and check his spaceship. If it's locked, use explosives. Take Caldwell with you.'

'Caldwell?' said Morgan. He had come to think of Caldwell as not to be trusted: all too often Caldwell had said a good word for the colonists. Morgan knew that to do his job properly he had to hate the colonists.

'I said, take Caldwell.' Dent did not like his orders being questioned. 'He's our mining expert—he knows how to use explosives.'

Morgan had noticed the sting in Dent's voice. 'Yes, sir,' he said, 'right away, sir.' He hurried off, pushing by two IMC guards who held between them a colonist prisoner.

'Sir,' said one of the guards, 'this is the man you particularly wanted to see.'

Dent looked at the frightened face of the colonist. It was the man who had hit Dent in the face when Dent was trussed to his own captain's chair in the IMC ship. 'You hit me,' said Dent. The man was too terrified to speak. 'And now I can do what I like with you.' He raised his handgun and pointed it straight at the man's head.

'No!' shouted Ashe. 'That's plain murder!'

But Dent had had no real intention of shooting the man. Slowly he lowered his gun. 'Why should I waste a single bullet, when you'll all soon be in that rickety old spaceship of yours, and die together?'

20

The Doomsday Weapon

Caldwell and Morgan walked well away from the scarlet spaceship, then both lay down flat on the ground to avoid the blast. They had tried battering on the hatch of the spaceship, but there had been no response from inside. Then they had tried to break it open with long-handled hatchets, but the hatchets had broken. Now Caldwell had smeared plastic explosive all round the hatch.

'If this doesn't do it,' said Caldwell, 'nothing will. Here goes.' He pressed the button of the remote-control detonator. There was a violent flash of flame, followed by the roar of the explosion. Both men got up and walked back to where the smoke was clearing.

'I hear you checked over the colonists' spaceship for them,' said Morgan.

Caldwell nodded. 'The least I could do.'

'Do they stand a chance?' asked Morgan.

'If they can ever get into free flight,' said Caldwell. 'But the whole thing's more likely to blow itself to pieces during take-off.'

'Then I'll stand well clear,' said Morgan, and laughed.

'You really hate colonists, don't you?' said Caldwell.

'I hate misfits,' said Morgan. They were now at the spaceship's hatch. The explosives hadn't even made a mark on the surface. 'I can't believe it,' said Morgan. 'Your sure you used real explosives?'

But Caldwell was staring at the key on the ground by his foot, and now picked it up. 'Why should anyone leave this lying around?' he said, and tried it in the lock. It turned easily, and Caldwell opened the door. Morgan went in first, then stopped dead.

'The size of this place,' said Morgan in wonder. He shook his head, as though uncertain whether he was imagining things. 'It's bigger inside than out!'

Caldwell had already seen Jo standing up in the glass box, waving frantically. He hurried across to her, walking straight through the beam of the burglar alarm.

.   .   .   .   .

The Doctor and the Master had reached the end of the trail that led to the Primitives' underground city. The Master stared at the face of rock. 'Well,' he said, 'how do we get in?'

'I haven't the remotest idea,' said the Doctor truthfully.

'Come now, Doctor,' said the Master, effecting his most charming smile, 'we haven't come all this way just to look at a face of rock? Show me how this rock opens.'

'I think it's keyed by thought waves,' said the Doctor. 'But I've no idea how to do it. Perhaps you should have considered this possibility before you insisted on my coming with you.'

The Master's smile was fast fading. 'Is there some other way in?'

'Very likely,' said the Doctor, 'but I don't know that either.'

'You're hardly being helpful, Doctor.' The Master tapped the pocket containing the little black box. 'I only have to touch the red button and Miss Grant will be dead within a few seconds . . .'

And at that moment the bleep-bleep sound came from the black box. Puzzled, the Master reached into his pocket, brought out the little box and opened its flap. On the miniature television screen he saw Caldwell breaking open the glass cubicle containing Jo. In sudden anger the Master put his finger on the red button. But at that moment the Doctor took advantage of the Master's distraction. With a high kick, he sent the little black box flying out of the Master's hand. With one hand stinging from the kick, the Master leapt backwards and at the same time whipped out his handgun. But the Doctor had anticipated this, and flung himself at the Master's legs. The two of them fell to the ground, the Doctor struggling to gain possession of the gun. All at once the gun was lifted from the Master's hand by the hand of a Primitive. The Doctor and the Master looked up. From the darkness, Primitives had appeared and were now surrounding them, their spears raised.

.　　　.　　　.　　　.　　　.

Jo was brought into the colonists' dome between Morgan and Caldwell. The place was filled with colonists each carrying some small item of tattered luggage. Dent was shouting at the armed IMC guards: 'These people are taking too much time. Keep them moving!' The guards started to herd the people down one of the corridors, the one that led to the entrance of their old spaceship. Then Dent noticed Jo. 'Where did you find her?' Caldwell explained. Dent showed little interest in why Jo had been a prisoner. 'What about that fake Adjudicator,' he asked; 'that's what I sent you for!'

'I think he wanted the Doctor to take him to the Primitives' underground city,' said Jo.

Dent looked puzzled. 'What's she talking about?'

'She tried to explain to us,' said Morgan. 'I can't make head nor tail of it. But if they've gone off there, they'll probably be killed by those savages.'

'Maybe,' said Dent. 'I'll send a squad of men after them once we've got rid of these characters,' and he indicated the colonists. 'Now Morgan, I want to get things *moving.*'

'Yes, sir,' said Morgan, and hurried away. Within a moment he was chivvying the colonists, hitting those who weren't moving fast enough.

'What about the girl?' Caldwell said.

Dent was about to move away. 'Oh, shove her in with the colonists,' he said, then went to help the guards herd the people down the corridor.

'I've got to stay here,' Jo pleaded. 'We've got to find the Master and stop him.'

'The who?' said Caldwell.

'You call him the Adjudicator,' she said, 'but he's really called the Master. He's a sort of super-criminal.'

'Oh, sure,' said Caldwell, scoffing. 'Any more stories like that?'

Jo looked up at Caldwell. 'Why don't you stop being so stupid?'

Caldwell was amused at being spoken to like that. 'You're a very cheeky young woman, you know.'

'It's time someone showed some sense,' Jo went on. 'The Master killed the real Adjudicator and took his place. There must be some reason for that, mustn't there?'

'I suppose so,' said Caldwell. 'Go on.'

'There's something in that Primitive city that's tremendously important,' Jo said. 'Can't you understand that?'

'You heard what Captain Dent said,' Caldwell answered. 'He's going to send a squad of our men later on.'

'Later on may be too late,' said Jo. 'Have you got anything to do right now, apart from herding those poor people on to that old spaceship?'

'I've got no part in that,' Caldwell said quickly.

'Then how about doing something useful?' she said. 'The two of us could find out what the Master's really after.'

Caldwell took a quick look round. The place was cleared now of colonists, and both Morgan and Dent had gone out of sight driving the colonists down the corridor. 'There's a buggy outside,' he said. 'Let's go.' The two of them hurried out into the night.

Dent, Morgan, and some IMC guards returned from their efforts of packing the colonists into the old spaceship. Dent said, 'I didn't see that hothead Winton get on the ship.'

'We'll search for him right away,' said Morgan.

But Dent checked him. 'Forget it. There's bound to be a few we missed out. We can pick them off at our leisure. I want all IMC personnel well clear of this area in case that old ship blows up while it's still on the ground.'

'If we aren't here,' said Morgan, 'what's to stop the colonists getting out of the ship and spreading all over the place again?'

Dent thought about that. 'Plant one guard with night binoculars on the nearest hill. Have him keep an eye on the spaceship from a safe distance until it takes off— or disintegrates on the ground!'

As Morgan and Dent moved away, Winton emerged from behind some sacks of seed and hurried out of the dome into the darkness.

. . . . .

The Doctor was once more a prisoner in the underground room with the frieze that told the story of the planet; but this time his companion was the Master.

'I thought you could communicate with these Primitives,' said the Master.

'They didn't hurt us,' answered the Doctor. 'Under the circumstances I thought they were quite pleasant.'

'Quite pleasant?!' The Master rubbed a bruised shoulder. 'They were extremely rough.'

'At least they didn't kill us,' said the Doctor. 'And they had the sense to relieve you of your gun.'

The loss of the gun obviously worried the Master. To cover his concern he turned to the series of wall pictures. 'Don't you think this is fascinating, Doctor? The whole story of the planet is here.'

The Doctor took another look at the crude pictures. 'If it is, perhaps you'd be good enough to explain it to me.'

'Delighted,' said the Master. 'This underground city was once the centre of a great civilisation. Through genetic engineering they developed a super-race.'

'The ones in long robes,' said the Doctor, 'with animal faces?'

'That's right . . .' The Master was about to continue, but the Doctor interrupted :

'You've deduced all that from these pictures?'

'Gracious no,' said the Master. 'It was all in the files of the Time Lords, which I was able to acquire.'

'Why are you so interested in the history of this planet?' asked the Doctor.

'This super-race,' said the Master, 'developed a super-weapon. Then some degeneration set in in the life strain, and they never used it.'

'I see,' said the Doctor, the pictures now making more sense to him. 'And the super-race have become the priests of a lunatic religion that serves machines which they think of as gods?'

'Something like that,' said the Master.

'Well, I think I should remind you that this religion included sacrifice,' said the Doctor, 'and my guess is that we are the intended victims.'

'Surely two brains such as ours,' said the Master, 'can overcome that problem, especially when the Doomsday Weapon, as it is called, is within our grasp.'

'What do you hope to do with this weapon?'

The Master pulled at his beard, contemplating the prospect. 'There may never be any need to use it. The mere threat of its use can hold the whole galaxy to ransom.'

The Doctor said, 'How did you know that these awful IMC people would be coming to this planet?'

The Master was about to answer as the door slowly opened. The Doctor noticed that the Master's hand quickly slipped into his tunic pockets, although he had no gun there now. The long-robed creature with the otter face slowly entered, followed by a phalanx of Primitives.

'Perhaps I should have mentioned,' the Doctor told the Master, 'that I'm known in these parts. I got away with my life once, but it certainly won't happen again.'

But the Master wasn't listening. 'We come in peace and friendship,' he said loudly to the otter face. 'I wish to talk with the Guardian of the Doomsday Weapon.'

As the priest stared at the Master blindly, the Master's hand suddenly came from his pocket clutching a handful of tiny silver capsules which he threw on to the floor. With his other hand he produced a gas-mask and held it to his face. As the capsules cracked on the floor each emitted a cloud of gas. The Primitives clutched their throats, choking for air, eyes streaming with tears, and the priest wheeled round in circles screaming. 'This way,' said the Master to the Doctor through his gas-mask, 'and *do* try to hold your breath.'

As the Master hurried out of the room he saw that one of the choking Primitives now had his gun attached to a waist-band. The Master ripped it off the band, then rushed out of the room. The Doctor, covering his mouth and nose with a handkerchief, hurried after him.

Escaping the gas and the the demented Primitives, the Master ran blindly down one corridor after another, the Doctor on his heels. Finally, the Master stopped and removed his gas-mask. He kept his gun aimed at the Doctor.

'You realise,' said the Doctor, 'that if they catch us now they will certainly kill us?'

'Then let us avoid being caught,' said the Master. With his free hand he produced from a pocket a tattered old map and studied it carefully. 'I think we are very near to our goal.'

'Since I've been no use to you up to now,' said the Doctor, 'why do you want me to come along?'

The Master gave his most charming smile. 'The company down here is so boring,' he said, 'and at least we understand each other. Now you read the map while I hold the gun on you so that you don't desert me in this gloomy place.' He gave the map to the Doctor; it showed the many corridors, rooms and galleries in the underground city. Over the square indicating one room a big X had been drawn. 'There's where we're making for,' said the Master. 'I don't think it should be too difficult for a fellow of your intelligence to lead us there.'

With the Master's gun pressed lightly in his back, the Doctor had no option but to try to steer their way through the maze of corridors. Very soon the Doctor recognised the corridors as those where he and Jo had been taken when they met the Guardian. On turning a final corner they could see at the dead-end of a corridor the huge double-doors and two Primitives standing guard.

'Is that it?' asked the Master.

'Yes,' said the Doctor, 'and it's guarded.'

The Master stroked his beard, thinking. 'This raises an interesting problem. If I raise my gun to shoot first one guard and then the other, then the gun cannot be pointing at you.'

'True,' said the Doctor.

'And you,' said the Master, 'could knock it out of my hand.'

'I would try to do it without hurting you,' said the Doctor.

'Nonetheless,' said the Master, 'using your Venusian karate you would soon render me unconscious, and then try to take me prisoner. Of course, I could let you run away at this point, and that would leave me free to deal with those two guards.'

'To murder them, you mean,' said the Doctor.

'What are the lives of two savages,' said the Master, 'compared with the value of bringing peace and order to the whole galaxy? Still, you always were sentimental, Doctor.' He paused to give the problem more consideration. 'I'm afraid there's only one practical solution. Regrettably I must shoot you first, then very quickly pick off the two guards before they have time to move.'

'Or,' said the Doctor, 'we might simply ask the two guards to go away.'

'How? They don't seem to understand anything we say.'

'By telepathy,' said the Doctor. 'I'm sure that's how they communicate, and how the priests give them their orders. May I ask them to go away on your behalf?'

'Is this some trick?' The Master held the gun menacingly close to the Doctor's head.

'In a sense, but not one aimed against you. Certainly among humans,' said the Doctor, 'telepathy takes place when two people's minds give off alpha waves at a cyclic rate between 9 and 11 per second. If I can find the cyclic rate of these Primitives, I can order them to leave that door unguarded.'

This appealed to the Master's intellect. 'All right,' he said, 'have a go. Let's see what you can do.'

The Doctor stared down the long corridor where the Primitives guarded the huge doors. He knew it was no use putting his command into words in his mind, for the Primitives might not understand. Instead he forced into his imagination a picture of the two guards laying down their spears and walking away from the big doors. He repeated this picture over and over again in his mind as he struggled to control his own brain to transmit only alpha thought-waves at the correct rate per second. To blot out from his mind that the guards were still standing by the door, he closed his eyes, then again repeated the mental picture.

'One of them moved!' whispered the Master. 'You're getting through.'

The Doctor tried again, this time at a much higher rate per second. The Master jogged his arm and he opened his eyes. 'Look,' said the Master excitedly. 'They're going!'

The two Primitives had put down their spears, and now they were slowly walking down the corridor towards where the Doctor and the Master were hiding. The Doctor and the Master pressed themselves back into an alcove, and the two Primitives slowly walked by them like sleep-walkers. When they had gone well out of sight the Master tugged at the Doctor's sleeve. 'Come on, you go first.'

The huge doors were not locked and were quite easy to open. The Doctor was back once more in the room whose walls were made of silvery-coloured metal. The Master looked about himself in satisfaction. 'The Doomsday Weapon,' he said; 'the most powerful weapon in the entire universe.'

'You mean that thing?' The Doctor indicated the drum-like object in the middle of the floor.

'This whole room,' said the Master, 'and the hundreds of miles of corridors of electronic equipment that stem from this room. It is *all* the Doomsday Weapon. That,' and he pointed to the construction in the middle of the floor, 'is the control console.' He went to the console and gently ran his fingers over the controls. 'With this in our control, we can rule all life on every planet in every galaxy.'

'We?' said the Doctor.

'Of course,' said the Master. 'Are we not both Time Lords? Isn't it our destiny to work together as partners?'

The Doctor heard sounds coming from the corridor. 'I think it may shortly be our destiny to die together if we're caught in here.'

The huge doors slowly started to open. 'Over here,' said the Master, waving his gun at the Doctor. There was nowhere in the room to hide, so the two of them took up a position with their backs to the wall close to the doors. The Master kept his gun at the ready. The huge doors continued to open, and then ten or more of the otter-faced priests entered. The Master and the Doctor stood there in wonder to see what the priests were about to do.

.   .   .   .   .

Using their buggies for quick transport, Captain Dent and the IMC men were now 35 safe kilometres away from the colonists' spaceship. Only one IMC guard re-

'With the Doomsday Weapon in our control,' said the Master, 'we can rule all life . . .'

mained near, a volunteer who was sitting lookout on a hill near the colonists' dome, using night binoculars for any sign of the colonists leaving their craft. Once back in his ship, Captain Dent went straight to the control room and sat comfortably in his captain's chair. He turned to the radio microphone.

'*Captain Dent to colonists' spaceship,*' he said. '*Do you hear me?*'

There was a crackle of static, then Ashe's voice. '*We hear you, Captain Dent.*'

'*What's delaying you?*' said Dent.

'*An electrical fault in our life-support system,*' said Ashe. '*We are just completing repairs.*'

'*Good,*' said Dent. '*Then get off this planet!*'

He switched off the microphone. Morgan had come up behind him. 'That's a laugh,' said Morgan. 'They don't need a life-support system, not if that old crate is going to blow itself to pieces!'

Dent turned on the microphone again, and tuned into the IMC guards' frequency. *'Captain Dent here,'* he said into the microphone, *'speaking to lookout guard. Any sign of movement around that old spaceship?'*

The guard's voice came back clearly. *'No, sir. Their hatch remains closed. No one's tried to leave the ship.'*

'Keep watching,' said Dent. *'If that hatch opens one millimetre, tell me immediately.'*

'Yes, sir,' said the guard's voice.

Dent switched off the microphone, leaving the wavelength open for incoming transmissions. He thought for a moment, then turned to Morgan: 'Get the men ready to go over to that so-called Primitive City.'

'Couldn't it wait till daylight?' said Morgan. 'Once that old ship's taken off, there's only us and that fake Adjudicator and that Doctor man left on the planet. We can wipe them out in no time.'

'I want everything finished and done with tonight,' said Dent. 'By first light I want to radio IMC Headquarters on Earth and tell them to send in the heavy mining gear, and I want to be able to report that this planet is entirely clear of everyone. So get moving!'

'Yes, sir,' said Morgan, and hurried out to get ready the guards.

Captain Dent sat thinking. Then he turned the ship's external television eye in the direction of the sky over the colonists' dome and spaceship. He hoped that very soon he would see the glare of the colonists' ship taking off on its last journey.

. . . . . .

The IMC guard acting as lookout crouched on top of the little hill overlooking the colonists' spaceship, his night binoculars piercing the darkness as he watched the hatch of the ship. He was cold and the rocky surface was too uncomfortable to sit on. He had volunteered for the job because it would be recorded in his personnel file, and he earnestly wanted to become a First Officer so that he would get a bigger living unit on Earth. His arms ached through trying to hold the binoculars with one hand and his high-powered rifle with the other. Then he questioned why he was holding the rifle, since all the colonists were in their spaceship. He put the rifle down, and now he was able to use both hands to hold the heavy binoculars. Almost as soon as he had put down the rifle, Winton sprang at him from the darkness, battering at him with a knife-sharp rock.

·   ·   ·   ·

Jo stood by while Caldwell fixed one of the front wheels of the buggy. In the darkness they had hit a rock, knocking out the track of the buggy's steering gear. More than once they had lost track of the footprints and track marks that were guiding them to the entrance of the Primitives' underground city. Caldwell straightened up.

'That should be all right,' he said. 'Get back on.'

As Jo climbed on the seat next to Caldwell they both heard the distant roar of the old spaceship's rocket motors. They turned and looked. The spaceship rose slowly into the night sky, a downthrust plume of flame lifting it higher and higher.

'Well,' said Caldwell, starting up the buggy, 'they made it.' He grinned with relief, and the buggy began to move slowly forward.

All at once a brilliant flash lit all the land around them like daylight. It was followed by a momentous explosion as the colonists' spaceship disintegrated.

Caldwell stopped the buggy. He was unable to speak.

'All those poor people,' said Jo.

'Yes,' said Caldwell at last. 'All those poor people. Dead.'

He started the buggy again and they drove ahead slowly and in total silence.

·   ·   ·   ·

The Doctor and the Master stood with their backs pressed to the silvery-coloured wall as two more priests entered carrying with them a casket. 'If you play your telepathy trick,' whispered the Master, 'and warn them of our presence, I shall shoot you instantly.'

'If they know of our presence,' whispered the Doctor, 'there will be no need for you to shoot me. We shall both be killed.'

The priests all made a ritual bow to the drum-like control console in the middle of the room. Then they turned towards the hatch in the wall and opened it. Heat from the furnace inside filled the room. Two priests went forward with the casket, a third with long tongs. The lid of the casket was removed and the L-shaped ends of the tongs were dipped into the casket. When the tongs were lifted, they gripped an isotope—fuel for a nuclear reactor. The priest slowly thrust the isotope deep into the white hot furnace.

The Master whispered, 'They must be refuelling the weapon.'

'My guess,' whispered the Doctor, 'is that it's a religious ceremony with a scientific basis. It must have been going on for generations.'

The otter faced priests slowly backed away from the now closed hatch, and backed out through the two, huge doors. The doors were closed from the outside. The Master moved away from the wall: 'Now, Doctor,' he said, very reassured again, 'let us see what the Dooms-day Weapon can do.' He inspected the controls on top of the drum-shaped console, then pressed one of the buttons. The colour of the whole of the wall on one side of the room changed from silvery grey to dark blue and then to black. Little spots of light appeared. 'How ingenious,' said the Master; 'before our eyes, the galaxy.' He turned a calibrated knob on the control console, and the little spots of light started swimming towards them at enormous speed. The picture of the galaxy was focussing down to one particular spot of light in the centre. After some moments this central spot of light had increased from a spot to a small white disc. Now the Master touched another control and the picture of the galaxy settled and stopped moving. 'That disc,' said the Master, 'is the sun of the planet Earth that you're so fond of. As you know, that sun will eventually burn through to its own core and explode—in about ten thousand million years' time. But with this weapon I can set that motion in progress now.'

'To what purpose?' asked the Doctor. 'Sheer destruction?'

'Doctor,' said the Master somewhat hurt, 'have you ever known me to be vindictive?' He continued before the Doctor had time to answer. 'Naturally the weapon will never be used provided people obey my commands. But to achieve this end, I need your help. The weapon is complex, it needs intelligent minds to operate it. So think of it, Doctor—a half-share in the Universe.' He stepped back and again levelled his gun at the Doctor. 'What is your decision?—to accept my generous offer, or instant death?'

'There will be no decision.'

The voice came from the furnace. Both the Doctor and the Master whirled round to look as the hatch slowly opened. Floating up from the flames was the Guardian. It pointed a finger at the Master's gun and instantly he dropped the gun and grabbed at his burnt hand. The gun turned white with heat where it lay on the floor, then melted.

'There will be no decision,' the Guardian repeated, 'because now you must both account to me. Do not try to run away. For you, there is no escape.'

. . . .

Caldwell shone a strong torch on to the face of rock at the end of the trail. 'They took you through this rock?'

'It opens somehow,' said Jo. 'But I don't know how.'

'Maybe we've found the wrong section of rock,' said Caldwell.

'No, it was definitely here. Anyway, look at all these

footprints.' From the spill of light from Caldwell's torch Jo could see many footprints all around them.

Caldwell shone the torch on to the ground, and scratched his chin. 'Yes, you're right. Some of them seem to lead straight into the rock. How about looking round for another entrance somewhere?'

Jo didn't like this idea because there was no certainty of ever finding another way into the Primitives' city. But she didn't want to disagree with Caldwell too much in case he decided to get back on to the buggy and return to the IMC ship. 'All right,' she said, 'so long as we find the Doctor.'

They got back onto the buggy. Caldwell was just about to start it when the rock began to open. Jo exclaimed: 'Look!' But Caldwell was already off the buggy and hurrying round to stand flat against the rock next to where it was opening. The rock door continued to open and a Primitive stepped out. Caldwell edged along the rock, then clenched his right fist, raised it, and brought it down like a hammer on the back of the Primitive's head. The Primitive fell forward, sprawling in the dust.

'Quick!' Caldwell grabbed the rock door to stop it from closing again. Jo leapt off the buggy and rushed into the entrance, followed by Caldwell. The rock door closed shut behind them. They looked down the long corridor cut through the rock.

'Where now?' said Caldwell.

'I don't know,' said Jo truthfully. 'This is where the search really begins.'

.   .   .   .   .

The Guardian addressed itself to the Doctor. 'Why have you returned?'

'I was brought here against my will,' said the Doctor.

The Master still couldn't believe his eyes. 'What is it?' he asked the Doctor quietly. 'How can it live in that heat?'

'I think it's the ultimate development of life on this planet,' the Doctor whispered.

'You,' said the Guardian, looking at the Master, 'what do you want here?'

The Master smiled. 'To restore this city and this planet to their former glory. You have here a wonderful invention. With it we can bring peace and order to every inhabited world in the Universe. Your planet will be the centre of a mighty empire, the greatest the cosmos has ever known.'

'This invention,' said the Guardian slowly, 'has destroyed us. Once the weapon had been built our race began to decay. The radiation from its power source poisoned the soil and even the upper atmosphere.'

'Exactly,' said the Doctor. 'The weapon has only brought death.' He pointed at the Master. 'This man wants to spread that death throughout the Universe Only you can stop him. You must destroy the weapon.'

'I am the Guardian of the weapon, and its radiation gives me life.'

'Then I am afraid,' said the Doctor, 'you must give up your own life so that others may survive.'

'Don't listen to such rubbish,' said the Master. 'You can continue to live, and I shall protect you! With the Doomsday Weapon, I shall protect all the Universe.'

'Against what,' said the Guardian, 'will you protect the Universe?'

The question took the Master off balance. 'Well,' he said, 'against anyone who tries to attack it.'

'But the Universe is all matter in Space,' said the Guardian. 'So what can attack that which is everything?'

'I . . . I shall protect it against itself,' said the Master, desperately wishing to get out of this discussion. 'I shall protect it against evil-doers.'

The Guardian said nothing for some moments. Then, it spoke again, 'The price is too high, the risk too great. The weapon is too terrible to be under the control of any creature that might use it.'

'Surely it is under your control?' said the Master, who clearly now doubted whether the Guardian actually controlled the weapon.

'No,' said the Guardian. 'I am only the Guardian. I have the power, as you saw, to destroy that small metal weapon with which you menaced your companion, but I have no power to destroy you. The controls of the Doomsday Weapon are at your side, there for you to command.'

The Master looked at the control console. 'Then I am now the master of the Universe,' he said. He strode over to the controls filled with a sense of victory and total power. 'That planet you so favour,' he said to the Doctor, 'the one called Earth, can become a cloud of ashes at my touch. Even the Daleks will tremble when they know my power!'

'But this is not to be,' said the Guardian. It turned to the Doctor. 'This man proves you are right. The Doomsday Weapon is not only evil, but it creates evil in others. It must be destroyed. And therefore I must die.'

The little doll-like figure of the Guardian began to fade back into the flames. The Master swung round to the open hatch. 'Just a minute,' he shouted, 'you and I can make an arrangement. I didn't *really* mean to use the weapon, only to frighten a few worlds.' The Guardian was already only half visible in the flames. 'Please come back,' screamed the Master. 'I am very clever. I may be able to restore you to the creature you were before you got so small and lived in those flames.' Only the head of the Guardian was now visible. 'Let's discuss this a little longer! Please don't go away!' But the image of the Guardian had now vanished completely. The Master turned away from the hatch, angry that he had shown himself so upset in front of the Doctor. 'Well,' he said, 'I've still got the Doomsday Weapon. Do you wish to share it with me?'

'I somehow think,' said the Doctor, 'that very shortly there will be nothing to share...'

The Doctor's words were swamped by a terrible roaring sound from within the furnace. A blistering wave of heat swept out from the hatch. Then the first sheet of flame burst from the hatch. The whole room started to tremble! The Master stared unbelieving at the now belching furnace. 'You fool,' he screamed, 'you're destroying yourself! You're destroying the Doomsday Weapon!'

'And it'll destroy us if we don't get out of here,' said the Doctor. Another great sheet of flame burst from the furnace. The room trembled violently and a huge crack appeared down one of its silvery-coloured metal walls. 'If you don't mind, I'm leaving before we get roasted to death. I suggest you do the same.'

The Doctor ran to the doors, then realised the Master was not following him. He turned back to see the Master still staring at the furnace as though mesmerised. 'Come on, man,' he called, 'you'll be killed!' The room trembled again as in an earthquake. Flames were now bursting from the furnace. 'We've got to get away!' called the Doctor.

The Master turned to him. 'The Doomsday Weapon,' he said, 'it will never be mine.' Then he followed the Doctor. As they left the room flames spewed out from the hatch engulfing the control console.

As they ran down the first corridor the floor was quaking, the rock walls trembling. 'Which way?' called the Master. They came to an intersection which the Doctor thought he recognised. 'This way, I think,' said the Doctor, and kept running. The Master kept up behind him. There was no sign of any otter faced priests or the Primitives. Cracks started to appear in the rock walls and roof. Boulders of rock fell from the roof as they ran down one corridor after another. They came to another point where the corridor split into different directions. The Doctor stopped. 'You had a map—give it to me.' The Master handed over the map, his hand trembling with fear.

'Doctor!' It was Jo, running down one of the corridors towards them, Caldwell behind her. 'Are you all right?'

'None of us is all right,' said the Doctor, trying to read the map and understand it, 'not while we're down here.'

'What's happening?' said Caldwell.

'I think the whole place is going to explode,' said the Doctor. He looked up from the map. 'I think we may find an exit this way.' He grabbed Jo's arm and started running again. As they left the spot, the rock wall fell in.

Two minutes later they came to a small opening in the rock face. It opened on to a circular staircase cut in the rock. The Doctor stopped, again checking the map. 'This could be it.'

'As long as those stairs lead up,' said Caldwell, 'that sounds good to me. Come on!' He bounded up the steps, the others following. From behind they could hear massive underground explosions. Caldwell got well ahead, and soon they heard his voice from above. 'It's all right—we're in the open!' A moment later they were all emerging from a hole in the rock. They had come up into the open inside a devil's playground of huge rocks and boulders. It was still night, but already the sun's rays were lighting the western sky. Even here the rock beneath their feet was slightly trembling. 'We'd better get away from here,' said Caldwell. 'We've got to find the buggy. I reckon we go this way.' He walked off quickly, the others following.

'So much for your interest in science,' said the Master, hurrying along behind the Doctor and Jo. 'The most powerful machine ever created in the Universe, and you let that fool Guardian destroy it all.'

'Science like that,' said the Doctor, 'is something we can all do without.'

Captain Dent stepped out from behind a boulder, his gun raised. 'Stop!' He signalled with his free hand. IMC men carrying their high-powered guns appeared from all sides. Dent turned to Caldwell. 'Thank you for leading them to us. Now stand over there.'

Caldwell stood speechless. Jo knew by his expression

that he had no knowledge of the ambush. Resigned, he walked over to the spot indicated by Captain Dent. The Master walked up to Dent.

'Congratulations, Captain Dent,' said the Master. 'You're just in time. Put these people under arrest.'

'Get back with your accomplices,' ordered Dent, and pointed his gun directly at the Master.

'You don't understand,' the Master protested, 'I'm the official Adjudicator, sent here by Earth Government.'

Morgan stepped forward, also armed. 'You're an impostor. Now get back.' He pushed the Master back in line with the Doctor and Jo. Then he turned to the IMC guards. 'All right, firing squad, step forward!'

Six IMC guards lined up in front of the Doctor, Jo, and the Master. They raised their guns, ready for the order.

'You're insane,' said Caldwell, speaking to both Dent and Morgan. 'You're murderers!'

Dent turned to him. 'Caldwell, if we didn't need you as our mining expert, you'd be over there with them. So shut up!' He turned to the IMC guards. 'Take aim!'

Suddenly Winton's voice called out from somewhere among the surrounding boulders. 'Drop those guns, all of you!'

Dent turned and fired wildly. All around colonists rose up from behind the boulders shooting at the IMC men. The Doctor grabbed Jo to pull her to safety. The IMC men fired at any colonist's head they could see appearing over the boulders. But they had to fire from crouching positions in the open, whereas the colonists all had the protection of the ring of great rocks. Morgan fell dead as a colonist's bullet hit him, and Captain Dent's gun was shot from his hand. Within moments half the IMC men were either dead or wounded.

'Surrender,' called Winton. 'You will not be killed.'

'We give in,' Dent shouted. He called to what remained of the IMC guards. 'Throw down your guns!'

The IMC men dropped their guns, and raised their

hands in surrender. Now, from all sides, colonists appeared from behind the boulders. Winton ran forward to the Doctor and Jo. 'Are you two all right?'

Jo let Winton help her to her feet. 'But the spaceship,' she said, 'it exploded.'

'Captain Dent left one lookout to make sure no one should escape by leaving the ship,' said Winton. 'I

They saw the Master's TARDIS as it raced into the dawn sky.

stayed behind and knocked him out. That let all the others get out of the ship to safety before it took off.'

'Did you make it take off by remote-control?' asked the Doctor.

Winton shook his head. 'No. John Ashe went up with it. He insisted on doing so. He gave his life for the sake of the rest of us.' He shrugged. 'Maybe he was a bit crazy.'

'Perhaps,' said the Doctor, 'or a saint.'

The Doctor's words were drowned by the thunder-clap roar of a spaceship in flight. Everyone looked up, and for a few seconds they saw the Master's TARDIS still looking like an Adjudicator's spaceship as it raced into the dawn sky.

'You let him get away!' said Jo.

'Ah, well,' said the Doctor, 'I suppose we all make mistakes sometimes.' He turned to Winton again. 'What are you going to do about your prisoners?'

'Send them back to Earth,' Winton said; but his attention was still focussed on the sky. 'Look, clouds!' He pointed to a formation of clouds that was sweeping in from the west. 'There have never been clouds like that before,' he said, 'not since we came here.'

The Doctor looked towards the oncoming clouds. 'You know something,' he said to Jo, 'I think it's going to rain.'

21

Mission Completed

The colonists stood in a circle around the big grave they had dug a little way from the main dome. Most of the IMC men had been safely locked up in their spaceship, ready to be sent back to Earth. But Captain Dent, Caldwell, and three guards were present at the ceremony to bury their own dead. Colonists and IMC guards killed in the final battle were laid side by side in the grave. Gentle rain fell from the clouds, soaking the colonist's poor clothing and making the dusty soil turn into mud. When all the bodies were in the grave everybody turned to Winton, expecting him now to speak as John Ashe had done before. He turned to the Doctor. 'You say something,' he pleaded.

'No,' said the Doctor, 'it has to come from one of you. This is your land now.'

Winton turned to face the colonists and the IMC men who stood sullenly as prisoners on the other side of the communal grave. 'I don't know how to make speeches,' he said, 'but I can tell you how I feel. Our people didn't die for nothing. To get anything worth having, like freedom, sometimes you have to fight, and sometimes you have to die. So now it's up to us to make this colony work, for the sake of the people who died.' He paused, then turned to the five IMC prisoners. 'Your people died for the wrong things, but I'm still sorry they got killed.' He looked down into the grave. 'There's one man missing—John Ashe. We can't bury him, but we can always remember him. He died so that we could live.'

No one spoke for a long time. They just stood, looking into the grave, remembering. Then the first man picked up some of the muddy soil and threw it into the grave, and each of the rest followed this ritual in turn.

Winton gave orders for the IMC prisoners to be escorted back to their spaceship. But Caldwell stepped forward from the IMC group. 'You've lost some good men,' he said to Winton. 'You're going to need more people to make this colony a success. I'm a good engineer. How about it?'

'We're going to declare an independent republic,' said Winton. 'Do you want to be an outlaw?'

Caldwell smiled. 'I told you, I'm a good engineer. You're going to need people like me.'

'All right. Let's go back to the dome and talk.' Winton led Caldwell away, and the two men slowly walked back towards the main dome.

.   .   .   .   .

In the dome Mary Ashe, Jo, and some of the other younger women had been busy preparing what food and drink they had for the others. As the colonists returned from the burial the Doctor detected the beginning of a more hopeful mood amongst them. He noticed that Winton and Caldwell were already discussing how to improve the structure of the dome, where to dig deep wells for more water. Then the men who had escorted the IMC prisoners to their ship returned, and one of them made immediately for the Doctor. 'That blue box you lost . . .' said the man, 'we found it on the way back here. It's in one of the old Primitive ruins.' He drew a crude map to show the way.

The Doctor thanked the man and then hurried over to Jo. 'I know where the TARDIS is. I think it's time to go.'

Jo was busy pouring tea for the others. 'But there are so many things to do here, Doctor. Are we in a hurry?'

'Stay if you want to,' he said to her. 'But I'll never be able to explain it to the Brigadier.'

Jo smiled. 'All right. I'll just say goodbye to everybody.'

The Doctor checked her. 'No. They'll all start asking where we came from again. Let's just slip out while they're enjoying their victory.' He took Jo's hand and together they went out of the dome. The rain had stopped now, and the sun was shining brilliantly.

'Look!' said Jo in wonder. 'It's all green!'

As far as the eye could see the one-time impoverished land was shooting up tiny blades of grass. Even the little shrub plants had grown new leaves.

'We'd better be quick getting to the TARDIS,' the Doctor laughed. 'The speed things can grow here, we may find ourselves having to cut through a jungle!'

They hurried away from the dome.

.   .   ◦   .   .

The Brigadier strode into the Doctor's laboratory at UNIT headquarters. 'Another false alarm,' he said as he entered. 'The man they thought was the Master turned out to be the Spanish Ambassador . . .'

He stopped because he realised he was talking to himself. Not only that, but the Doctor's precious police box was missing from its corner in the room.

'Doctor,' he called loudly, 'where *are* you?'

Even as he spoke he heard the strange heaving sound of the TARDIS returning. In a moment the TARDIS materialised once more in its corner. The door opened and the Doctor and Jo stepped out.

'What the devil are you two playing at?' said the Brigadier. 'Where have you been? I told you I'd be back within the hour.'

'Within the hour?' said Jo. 'But we've been away for days!'

'For *days*?' said the Brigadier in total disbelief. 'Miss Grant, I think you're losing your sense of time.'

'On the contrary,' she said with a smile. 'I think I'm just beginning to gain it.'

STAY ON

Here are details of other exciting TARGET titles. If you
cannot obtain these books from your local bookshop, or
newsagent, write to the address below listing the titles
you would like and enclosing cheque or postal order—
not currency—including 7p per book to cover packing
and postage; 2–4 books, 5p per copy; 5–8 books, 4p per
copy.

TARGET BOOKS,
Universal-Tandem Publishing Co.,
14 Gloucester Road,
London SW7 4RD

DOCTOR WHO AND THE DAY OF THE DALEKS   30p
Terrance Dicks
0 426 10380 7   **A Target Adventure**

Mysterious humans from 22nd century Earth 'time-jump'
back into the 20th century so as to assassinate a high-ranking
diplomat on whom the peace of the world depends. DOCTOR
WHO, Jo Grant and the Brigadier are soon called in to
investigate. Jo is accidentally transported forward to the 22nd
century; the Doctor follows, eventually to be captured by his
oldest and deadliest enemy, the DALEKS! Having submitted
the Doctor to the fearful Mind Analysis Machine, the DALEKS
plan a 'time-jump' attack on Earth in the 20th century!
Illustrated.

If you enjoyed this book and would like to have information sent you about other TARGET titles, write to the address below.

You will also receive:

A FREE TARGET BADGE!

Based on the TARGET BOOKS symbol—see front cover of this book—this attractive three-colour badge, pinned to your blazer-lapel, or jumper, will excite the interest and comment of all your friends!

and you will be further entitled to:

FREE ENTRY INTO THE TARGET DRAW!

All you have to do is cut off the coupon beneath, write on it your name and address *in block capitals*, and pin it to your letter. You will be advised of your lucky draw number. Twice a year, in June and December, numbers will be drawn 'from the hat' and the winner will receive a complete year's set of TARGET books.

Write to: TARGET BOOKS,
           Universal-Tandem Publishing Co.,
           14 Gloucester Road,
           London SW7 4RD

———————————— cut here ————————————

Full name...

Address..

....

.... County..

       Age...................................